Stealing Thunder

DAVID LEE CORLEY

Copyright © 2018 David Lee Corley
All rights reserved.

DEDICATION

To my brother, Michael John Corley, the anvil and hammer that forged my drive to succeed and the friend that I have come to accept, but will never fully understand.

ACKNOWLEDGMENTS

I would like to thank Antoneta Wotringer for her excellent book cover design. She is truly an artist with a unique sense of style. I would also like to thank JJ Toner for proofreading. He is by far better at spelling and grammar than me and an author himself.

ONE

It was late afternoon in the German forest. The shadows were long and the air was brisk. The woods were silent except for a boar using its tusks to root through dried leaves searching for a meal. It was autumn, and food was growing scarce.

The boar moved past an object about the size of a sports car sitting silently on the ground next to a fallen tree. Its outline was smooth without edges. It had a low profile and its color and pattern matched the surrounding foliage perfectly, making it hard to see. It appeared to be both part of the fallen tree and part of the leaf-covered ground. A weld line along one of its plates revealed that the object was metal. It had multiple panels with tight seal lines making them almost invisible. It didn't move and the boar ignored it, like some forgotten piece of junk left in the wild to rust.

In the distance, there was a faint grinding of metal gears. As the noise grew, the boar looked up, unhappy at being interrupted. He didn't like the mechanical sound. It was human, and he didn't like humans. He snorted and scampered off into the forest.

Three Leopard 2 tanks, marked with the German army insignia on their turrets, approached through the woods. The well-camouflaged Leopards were protected by sixty tons of advanced composite armor and 120-mm cannons. Considered by most experts to be the top main battle tanks in the world, the sleek Leopards were longer than the American M1 Abrams and the British Challenger tanks, with powerful, fifteen hundred horsepower engines. The Leopard's main mission was to fight off a Russian invasion should one occur, and the German tank commanders were confident they could defeat any Russian tanks that they might one day face.

The object sat motionless and silent as the tanks passed, unaware of its presence. As the sound of the mechanized patrol faded, a panel on top of the object opened and a 360-degree camera rose from the interior like a submarine periscope. The camera surveyed the forest.

Sitting in a control cockpit surrounded by video screens and electronics, was Staff Sergeant Lowell Gamble. His body was chiseled and his face weathered, showing his age. He was old for a staff sergeant. He looked around the screens to confirm that there were no German tanks in the area. "Victor Echo Six, this is Red Badger One. Clear. Over," he said in his radio headset.

"Red Badger One, this is Victor Echo Six. You are clear to engage. Weapons free. Over," said a woman's voice over the radio.

"Copy that, Victor Echo Six. Over," said Lowell keying in commands on a keyboard and operating the controls in the cockpit.

The object sitting on the forest floor unfolded into a windowless vehicle, rising up on four shock-absorbing arms with wide wheels on the ends, not unlike a four-legged spider on roller-skates. A long panel on top of the vehicle opened up and a short-barreled 120mm cannon emerged. To save space and weight, the cannon was not mounted on a turret. It used the vehicle's maneuverability to align its shots horizontally and the base of the cannon mount pivoted up and down to align its shots vertically.

On the barrel, the word "Thunder" was stenciled in white, an unauthorized addition to its adaptive camouflage. Thunder whipped a U-turn and sped off through the woods in search of its prey.

Equipped with an electric motor as its means of propulsion, Thunder drove silently through the trees except for a faint whine and the crunch of leaves beneath its wheels. As it moved through the forest, its reactive camouflage changed color and pattern to better match its surroundings giving it a ghost-like appearance.

Thunder came up behind the German tanks unnoticed; its approach masked by the Leopard tanks' grinding treads and loud engines.

Inside the control cockpit, Thunder's automatic targeting system identified each of the German tanks. Lowell used his joystick to select the first target - the Leopard tank on the far left of the line. "Thunder, load sabot," he said into his headset.

Thunder responded to Lowell's voice command and loaded a shell into the cannon's breach. As a safety precaution Thunder required a human to fire its weapons. "Sabot up," said a synthetic voice over the radio.

Lowell rechecked that the gunsight's crosshairs were centered on the back of the German tank and squeezed the trigger on the joystick.

Thunder's cannon fired with a loud crack. "Away," said the synthetic voice over the radio.
As the round left the barrel, Thunder automatically stooped down, flattening itself against the forest floor, it's reactive camouflage matching the surrounding foliage perfectly.

The German tank commander heard the crack of the cannon in the same instant the shell exploded smearing the rear of his tank with red paint. He cursed and threw off his headset.
The two remaining tank commanders searched the tree line for the enemy. Nothing was visible. The commanders radioed each other to coordinate their attack. The two Leopard tanks turned and moved back into the forest, leaving the tank that had been hit; it and its crew having been designated "KIA" by the field judges.

"This is Red Badger One. Tango Alpha destroyed," said Lowell over the radio.
"This is Victor Echo Six. Acquire Tango Bravo, Red Badger One," said the woman's voice.

"Wilco, Victor Echo Six," said Lowell.

Thunder popped up, giving away its hiding place, and sped off into the trees.

One of the two remaining German tank commanders spotted Thunder as it changed its camouflage pattern. He barked out orders to his crew. The tank's turret whipped around and the gunner gave Thunder the appropriate amount of lead as he sighted the moving target. He fired. The Leopard tank's main gun cracked as the shell left the barrel followed by a lick of flame and smoke.

Thunder slammed on its brakes, skidded to a stop across the leaf-covered soil and crouched down to minimize its profile. The German tank round whistled past the front of Thunder and exploded with blue paint as the shell slammed against a tree.

"Thunder, load sabot," said Lowell into his headset.

Another shell loaded into Thunder's gun breech. "Sabot up," said the synthetic voice.

Thunder rose up and spun around toward the tank that had just fired and was now reloading.

Lowell rechecked the sight and pulled the trigger on the joystick.

Thunder's cannon fired hitting the front of the German tank and smearing it with red paint. "Away," said the synthetic voice.

"This is Victor Echo Six. That's a front shot, Red Badger One," said the woman's voice, angrily. "Armor is too thick in the front of a Leopard tank. It doesn't count. Reacquire and engage the Tango Bravo, Red Badger One."

"Shit," said Lowell to himself not remembering his mic was live.

"What's that, Red Badger One?"

"Nothing, Victor Echo Six. This is Red Badger One. Affirmative on reacquire and engage Tango Bravo. Over."

Thunder jumped back up on its wheels and sped through the trees until the remaining tanks were nowhere in sight. It made a sharp ninety-degree turn and raced through the trees. After a quarter of a mile, Thunder made a wide-arcing U-turn and approached the German tanks on their right flank.

Lowell sighted the tank on the far right flank. "Thunder, load sabot," said Lowell.

The shell loaded into the gun's breach. "Sabot up," said Thunder.

Lowell rechecked the sight and pulled the trigger.

Thunder's cannon fired with a crack. "Away," said Thunder's synthetic voice over the radio.

The shell exploded with red paint smearing the side of the German tank.

"Victor Echo Six, This is Red Badger One. Tango Bravo destroyed. Over," said Lowell over the radio.
"Copy that, Red Badger One. Over," said the voice of the woman.

The last remaining German tank appeared from behind the tank that was just hit, its turret swinging around to engage Thunder. It was a race against time in which the weapon that fired first would most likely survive.

Thunder's auto-targeting system identified the new threat and centered its crosshairs on the German tank.

"Thunder, load sabot," said Lowell over the radio.

The shell loaded. "Sabot up," said Thunder.

There was no time to recheck the sight. Lowell squeezed the trigger and hoped for the best.

Thunder and the German tank fired at the same time. "Away," said Thunder.
Thunder crouched down at the last moment and the German tank's shell sailed over the top of its canopy.
Thunder's shell found its mark exploding on the side of the German tank and covering it with red paint.

Lowell sighed with relief and said, "Thunder, ceasefire main cannon."

The cannon lowered back into Thunder's body, and the panel closed.

"Victor Echo Six, this is Red Badger One, Tango Charlie destroyed. Over," said Lowell with a shit-eating grin.

"This is Victor Echo Six. Well done," said the woman's voice. "Return to base, Red Badger One. Over."

"On the way, Victor Echo Six. Red Badger One. Out," said Lowell.

The German tank commanders flipped off the American contraption as it turned and sped off through the woods.

Thunder raced through the forest with amazing speed and agility, dodging trees and rocks like a slalom skier.

Thunder burst from the forest tree line. A herd of red deer grazing in a meadow scattered on seeing the strange vehicle.

Moving to the edge of the meadow, Thunder approached the embankment of a wide river. It retracted its cannon and sensors and closed all of its external panels, sealing them tight. It slowed as it hit the edge of the embankment and drove down the steep slope to the river. It slipped under the water's surface and was fully submerged as it traversed the river, its knobby tires easily navigating the rocky bed of the river.

On the opposite bank, it emerged from the water and drove up the embankment. Back on level ground, the vehicle picked up speed.

Thunder pulled onto a gravel access road, lowered itself closer to the ground like a race car, and kicked up a cloud of dust as it reached its top speed of ninety miles-per-hour.

Thunder passed a group of engineers building a wooden bridge across the river under the watchful eye of their sergeant. The men stopped to stare at the strange looking vehicle. "Knock off the lollygagging and get back to work," said the sergeant. "Jesus H. Christ, it's like you've never seen a space alien before."

As Thunder approached the gate that separated the training area from the U.S. Army base, the two guards were advised over the radio of the vehicle's approach and raised the barrier. Thunder whizzed past the guards into the base.

Soldiers stopped and stared at the windowless vehicle as it weaved its way through the base, stopping at stop signs and generally obeying the speed limit.

It pulled to a stop in front of a cargo container with a door on the side and two large doors on the back.

Inside the cargo container, Lowell sat at Thunder's control cockpit - a series of camera monitors, digital gauges and electronic devices mounted in air-conditioned racks. He removed his headset, punched a code into the cockpit's keyboard and locked down the system. The camera monitors blinked off and the control panels went dark. He rose from his chair, stretched, and exited the control cockpit through the side door.

Outside the control cockpit container, Lowell was approached by a squad of Military Policemen led by a 21-year old Sergeant Esposito. "She's all yours, Sergeant Esposito," said Lowell.

"Roger that, Staff Sergeant," said Esposito. "You heading into town for a beer?"

"Not yet. Gotta debrief first. Otherwise, the Lieutenant will get her green panties in a bunch," said Lowell.

"Can't have that," said Esposito.

"Can't have what?" said Lieutenant Maggie Garza appearing from around the edge of the control cockpit container. Her short hair accentuated her high cheekbones and her tailored uniform pressed against her curvaceous figure. Garza was an Italian-American beauty with a commanding presence. The MP's and Lowell snapped to attention and saluted the young officer. "Sorry, Ma'am," said Lowell. "Didn't see you coming."

"And you never will, Staff Sergeant," said Garza. "That's the point."

"Yes, Ma'am," said Lowell.

"At ease," said Garza. The MPs and Lowell relaxed. "Well done, Staff Sergeant Gamble. The generals were impressed."

"Thank you, Ma'am."

"Get cleaned up and get yourself a coke. Debrief in my office in twenty minutes."

"Roger that, Lieutenant," said Lowell as he saluted her again and moved off.

Lowell was walking across the base, headed for his quarters when he saw a familiar face stepping out of a Humvee – Master Sergeant Craig Turner, ten years his senior. "Sergeant Turner?" said Lowell.

Turner spun on hearing Lowell's voice and immediately recognized the face of the younger Sergeant. "Sergeant Gamble? What the hell are you doing here?" Turner walked over and the two men shook hands.

"I'm on special assignment with DARPA. What about you?"

"3rd Armor's got an upcoming training exercise. I'm doing a little recon," said Turner. "It's good to see you, Sergeant. How long's it been?"

"Gotta be six or seven years. Look. I got a debriefing I gotta get to, but how about a beer later and we can catch up? I'm buying," said Lowell.

"Free German beer? Hell, yes."

"O-nineteen-hundred. There's a beer garden in Grafenwöhr's town square called, 'Thumbach Bierpalast'. You can't miss it."

"Don't forget your wallet. I'm real thirsty," said Turner as they shook hands again and moved off in different directions.

Inside an office, Lowell debriefed Garza by slamming her up against the wall, holding her wrists and kissing her on the back of the neck. She responded with a moan. Lowell released her wrists and moved to unbuckle her belt. The buckle was jammed. "Let me do it," said Garza, unbuckling the belt and unbuttoning her trousers.

Lowell turned her around to face him, knelt, pulled down her green panties and bit her just below her belly button. Her eyes opened wide and she pushed his head lower…

TWO

Grafenwöhr was a sleepy town in eastern Bavaria. The slow-flowing Thumbach river ran through the heart of the town and through Statdpark with its flat green grass and playground. Near the town square was an Evangelical chapel, white and well-maintained, like most things German.

Le Van Tien sat in a pew near the front of the chapel wearing jeans and a flannel shirt. Tall for a Vietnamese American, Tien was the great-granddaughter of James McGovern, the famous American fighter pilot that had fought for America and the Chinese in World War II and the French in the Indochina War. Nicknamed 'Earthquake McGoon' after the hulking character in the Lil' Abner comic strip, McGovern had died long before Tien was born, but her family had kept his memory alive by recounting his exploits to the younger generation. Tien was alone with her thoughts which were racing at the moment. It was always like that before a buy. Sometimes she thought in Vietnamese and sometimes in English. That's the way it was with Tien like she couldn't make up her mind to which culture she belonged. She grew up in California with her seven brothers and sisters. Money was tight. Even at a young age, she was expected to supplement her family's income whenever possible and worked on weekends at her family's nail salon. If she ever complained, her mother and aunts would start in with the stories of life in Vietnam and the dangerous exodus of her great-grandmother and grandmother when the war ended. That usually shut Tien up.

Two men entered the chapel from the rear entrance. "You're late," said Tien as the two men, one larger than the other and each holding a box, approached.

"You got our money?" said the larger of the two men.

"It's not your money until I get the product," said Tien.

"Whatever. Flash the cash or we are out of here."

"You first. Let's see what you brought."

The men opened the lids on the boxes revealing vials of morphine. "Nice," said Tien reaching into one of the boxes. But the men closed the lids before she could retrieve one of the vials. "Cash first," said smaller man.

"How do I know it's real?"

"It's real."

"I'm just supposed to believe you? Where did you get it?"

"We're not giving you our source."

"Then I ain't buying. That stuff has to be refrigerated, ya know?"

"Yeah, we know. It was in a refrigerator at the base hospital until an hour ago. It's fine."

"Doctor or nurse lift it?"

"Neither. Janitor. Head nurse let him into the meds vault so he could mop the floor. Someone spilled their coffee and it leaked under the door."

"Brilliant. Do you two work at the base?"

"Enough with the questions. We doing this or what?" said the larger man.

Tien reached behind the hymn book on the shelf on the back of the pew. She pulled out a fat envelope and handed it to one of the men. They counted the cash. "Happy?" said Tien.

Satisfied, they handed her the two boxes. "When do you want more?" said the smaller man.

"Five to ten," said Tien.

"Days?"

"Years. When you get out of prison," said Tien.

The sound of boots stomping echoed through the chapel. The two men turned to see a dozen MPs with pistols drawn entering the chapel from four different directions. When they turned back to Tien she had her pistol drawn and pointed at them. "You're both under arrest," she said, holding up her U.S. Army Criminal Investigations Division Special Agent badge. "And I'm gonna need the name of that janitor."

She could see the larger man searching for a way out as the MPs closed in. "You don't want to do that," said Tien. "I will shoot you."

The big man jumped up on to the bench and ran along the pew. Reaching the end, he jumped through a nearby window, crashing through the glass panes and wooden muntins. "Didn't see that coming," said Tien to herself.

"Arrest him," she shouted to the MPs pointing to the man still seated. She slipped her pistol in the holster on the back of her jeans, jumped up on the bench, ran along the pew and jumped through the window.

She landed outside the church and rolled across the cobblestones. She jumped up and looked around. The man ran down the street and ducked into an alley. She ran after him. She had no idea if he was armed or not, but wasn't taking any chances. She drew her pistol as she entered the alley.

It was almost sundown and the shadows were long as the sun hung low and shined straight in her eyes. *Bad angle,* she thought. There were empty crates stacked against the walls, broken shopping carts filled with junk, and dumpsters. The doors in the alley were recessed. Plenty of hiding places. She moved cautiously, checking each potential hiding place, keeping her distance, giving herself room to react. Several of the doorways were exits from restaurants and the ground was slippery from grease and liquid leaking from plastic trash bags.

She approached a dumpster and knelt. She looked under the dumpster and could see the man's shoes. "I can see your feet behind the dumpster," she said. The shoes moved. She knew it was him. "I'm gonna shoot you in the foot if you don't come out." The shoes didn't move. "Have you ever been shot in the foot? I hear it's really painful. All those little bones breaking, tendons snapping, not to mention the blood…"

"Okay, okay," said the man as he came out from behind the dumpster with his hands up.

"Lay down on the ground. Face down," she said.

"It's filthy. Look at all the grease," he said.

"Are you kidding me?" she said. "Get on the fucking ground."

He lay down. She put her knee on his back, pulled out a pair of handcuffs and cuffed him. Tien was not afraid of the man, but he had fifty pounds on her and she was not going to give him the chance to resist.

"Would you really have shot my foot?" he asked as she helped him to his feet.

"I don't know. Probably not. I had you pretty well boxed in," she said.

The man stumbled as he rose. She reached out to steady him. He leaned into her with all his weight pushing her against the dumpster. The dumpster rolled on its wheels. She lost her balance and fell. The man ran up the alley with his hands cuffed behind his back.

"Damn it," she said as she climbed to her feet, her clothes covered in grease. Tien had always been competitive and hated to lose at anything. She also had a keen sense of justice and loathed the idea that a criminal could escape after she had apprehended him. She leveled her pistol and took aim. The man made it to the end of the alley before she shot him in the left leg just below his buttocks. He went down.

"Oh, god. You shot me," said the man rolling on the ground in pain.

"I warned you not to run," she said. "It's your fault."

"I'm bleeding!"

"Yep. That's what happens when you get shot," she said, looking down at the bullet wound and the bloody spot spreading across the back of his pants.

The MPs from the church approached. "Radio for an ambulance," she said.

"I'm gonna die," the man said.

"No. You're not. But just in case..." She put her boot over the wound and put her weight on it. The man screamed in pain. The irony that he had stolen the very morphine that he would now need was not lost on Tien and she saw it as a kind of Karmic justice.

The MPs entered the alley and looked at the officer stepping on the wounded man on the ground. "What?" she said with a shrug. "I'm putting pressure on the wound. He's a bleeder."

THREE

Billy Gamble, Lowell's younger brother, hiked through Al Siq, an ancient passage formed from a split in the sandstone mountains of southern Jordan. The steep walls of the gorge were smooth from millions of years of erosion and the horizontal pink and orange layers of exposed rock gave the place an inviting feeling like a mother's womb. The sun peeked through the top of the gorge in shafts and formed pools light on the ground which he passed in and out of as he moved deeper into the mountain. It was beautiful and otherworldly.

He was alone, and that was the way he liked it. The only sound was the rhythmic echo of his cowboy boots bouncing off the stone walls. Most of the tourists had surrendered to the harsh afternoon heat and retired to their air-conditioned hotels in Wadi Musa, the hillside town just outside the national park.

Clumps of dark clouds blew in from the western mountains, blocking the sun and darkening the ancient passage, then releasing the sunlight moments later as they floated past. There were small niches carved in the walls - tiny stone temples to the block gods of the Nabataeans. The Nabataeans were a nomadic Arab tribe that controlled the area and its lucrative trading routes through the mountains. They had kept control for five thousand years and it had made them rich. They spent their wealth building the trading hub 'Raqmu,' now known as 'Petra.'

Billy heard a loud snort and the clomping of horseshoes on stone. A taxi cart carrying two overweight tourists and a Bedouin driver appeared. The taxi cart was a two-wheeled chariot with a colorful canopy, pulled by an Arabian horse. The small Arabian horses only averaged about 14 hands, but they were tough and fast, well known for their endurance, and often competed in the most grueling long-distance races.

Lowell, Billy's older brother, competed in Wyoming's Bighorn 100 when he was only seventeen after getting an age-waiver from the judges. The Bighorn was a 100-mile horse race through steep mountains, ice-cold streams, and unpredictable weather. Lowell didn't win, but just finishing gave him bragging rights and impressed the girls. Although he never would admit it, Billy was proud of his brother. Lowell was confident, tough and fearless, everything Billy wanted to be. But Lowell was also an asshole and Billy spent most of his childhood under constant threat of Lowell's unbreakable headlocks and painful noogies, not to mention his endless bragging. Later in life, Billy realized that his rugged character was forged from Lowell's hammer and anvil.

The taxi cart whizzed by and disappeared around a corner. Billy moved deeper into the gorge. It was still sunny when the first raindrop hit Billy's hand. It was a big one. He had seen drops like this before in Wyoming and Southeast Asia. Big drops meant big rain. He picked up his pace.

As he rounded a corner, the gorge walls grew dark in comparison to the bright shaft of light at the end of Al Siq. It took his eyes a moment to adjust and then he saw it... 'Al-Khazneh,' Bedouin for The Treasury. It was something he would never forget, which was saying a lot considering all the things he had seen in his four years of traveling the world. The ancient structure was carved into the rock face of a sandstone cliff and appeared white in the sunlight. It was built as the mausoleum of a Nabataean king and the Bedouin believed it contained treasures hidden behind its stone walls. The farther he moved toward the mouth of Al Siq, the wider the gap appeared and the more the Treasury was revealed, like a theatre opening its curtain. He stood transfixed in awe at the towering columns and skillfully sculpted facade, carved from the sandstone cliff face.

The grunt of a camel snapped Billy from his trance and he looked around. There were dozens of camels with colorful saddles laying on the ground waiting for tourists to board, but the tourists were gone. The Bedouin guides that rented the camels were busy packing up for the night. The day's business was over and the camels were hungry.

Three big raindrops hit Billy on his head and shoulders. *Here it comes*, he thought. Rain didn't bother him, but he didn't like to get his boots wet. Water would swell the leather and pull at the stitching. He could always find a pair of Levis blue jeans or even the flannel shirts he liked to wear almost anywhere in the world, but cowboy boots were a different matter. You could find a nice-looking pair of boots in most malls or tourist markets, but they were crap and would disintegrate before the end of the first year. A good pair of cowboy boots should last ten years or more, by Billy's reckoning. The key was to find a good cobbler that understood the unique construction of high-quality cowboy boots and could replace the leather soles and wooden heels when worn out. The leather had to be hand-stitched and lemon wood pegs used to pull the inner sole together with the outer sole. Billy's boots were Luccheses from El Paso, Texas, and not easy to find. Billy was not happy when a large raindrop splattered across the toe of his left boot. "Shit," he said to himself. "It's just a boot, Billy. It's just a boot."

Petra was built inside a narrow canyon and the Treasury was at the upper end of the canyon. He would need to hike lower into the canyon to see the other buildings. Billy knew he didn't have much time. He wasn't planning on staying in Jordan more than a day or two. There wasn't much to see in Jordan beyond Petra. He thought about renting a camel with a guide, but guides tended to drone on about the most mundane historical details. Billy was more of a big picture kinda guy and liked to explore on his own.

He skipped the camel tour and walked down the narrow passage known as 'The Street of Facades' that led from the upper canyon to the lower canyon. It began to rain in earnest.

A Bedouin guide shouted at Billy and made motions with his hands pointing at the sky. Billy ignored him. Having spent time in the Middle East, Billy knew the hustles of the Bedouin and wasn't in the mood. He marched on and disappeared around a canyon wall.

Billy made good time as he hiked past the ancient buildings and homes carved into the rock walls. In the lower canyon most of the tourists were gone and the guides with them. He unfolded the map the ticket agent at the main gate had given him. He hoped to see Ad-Deir, the stone-carved building known as 'The Monastery,' before it got too dark. It was located at the far end of the Petra city complex and up a steep hill. The hike didn't discourage him, but the dark clouds and the increasing rain was a bit disconcerting.

He walked about halfway when he realized that the rainwater was not running off like it would on a street or meadow. Instead, it was collecting on the hardened clay of the canyon floor. The water was rising. It had already risen past his ankles and would soon reach the top of his boots which were soaked all the way through. His socks were already drenched and his feet were getting cold.

Billy was stubborn, but not stupid. He turned and headed back the way he came. As he approached the Street of Facades, he recognized the source of the problem. The Street of Facades was gone and a muddy river running through the canyon had taken its place. There was another passage out of the canyon, but he imagined it would have the same problem; too much water on the hard packed canyon floor with no place to run off. The water on the lower canyon was rising quickly and he knew he had better get his ass to higher ground before the entire canyon became the world's largest swimming hole. The water pouring out of the upper canyon and into the lower canyon was moving fast.

He waded into the river that was once a street and the water quickly reached his crotch. His balls and penis shriveled from the cold water and he could feel the sand-filled water chaffing his inner thighs. He pushed up into the passageway as the canyon walls narrowed. It was slow going. The higher he climbed the narrower the canyon walls and the deeper the water. To make matters worse, the water was muddy and he couldn't see where he was stepping. The hard rain had broken loose several small boulders and carried them into the passage. He found them when he kicked them by accident. Even with his boots, his shins stung when they met a boulder head-on. It felt like bumping into a coffee table in the middle of the night.

There were two Jordanian Park Rangers in the upper canyon that saw him and waved him off fearing the rushing water would overtake him. The Jordanian Park Service had a limited budget which did not include fast water rescue training and the Rangers were unsure of what to do.

The rain was relentless and getting heavier. Billy pushed on, slowly moving up the river one step at a time. He knew he would make it to the upper canyon if he could just keep his balance and stay on his feet.

The Bedouin guide that had yelled at Billy earlier was on top of his camel and had a coil of rope. Billy watched him as the guide steered his camel into the river and prepared to throw the rope down to him. *That's more like it,* thought Billy as he planted his feet and prepared to grab the rope. The guide flung the rope, but the end bunched up and failed to uncoil all the way, landing short in the river. Billy moved slowly toward the end of the rope. The river was moving very fast now, and the water had reached his waist. Seeing that Billy was struggling to get to the end of the rope, the guide steered his camel down the passage and into deeper water. "No. No. Bad idea," said Billy waving at the guide to turn back.

Too late. The normally sure-footed camel lost its balance and toppled into the river. "Oh shit," said Billy as the camel and the guide headed straight for him. There was no time to get out of the way. Billy could see the guide didn't know how to swim and was grasping for the camel's reins like they were his only lifeline. The camel struggled to regain its footing while keeping its head above water. Billy saw what was going to happen next and took a deep breath. It was all he could do. *Death by camel* thought Billy. *Never would've guessed it.* The thrashing camel and the panicking guide plowed into Billy, knocking him off his feet and into the rushing water.

Billy protected his head from the camel's kicking feet. He knew if he was knocked unconscious he would drown before anyone could get to him. His body bounced along the bottom of the river smacking against boulders and scraping against the rocks and sand.

The guide decided Billy was a better life preserver than the thrashing camel and grabbed him around the neck, choking him. *Great,* thought Billy. He elbowed the guide in the face, breaking his nose. The guide let go and Billy was free. Unwilling to let the man drown, Billy wrapped his arm over the guide's shoulder, across his chest and grabbed the man's shirt under his armpit. He did his best to keep the man's head above water and away from the camel's feet.

As the river widened into the lower canyon, the camel stopped floating and regained its footing. This had the added advantage for Billy of not being kicked in the head. Billy and the guide floated past the camel as the animal headed back up river. Billy reached out and grabbed the camel's guide rope and wrapped it around his hand like a bull-rider wraps his saddle rope. Billy and the guide were dragged by the camel through the passage and into the upper canyon. Safe, Billy released the rope and climbed to his feet. Disregarding his master's shouts, the camel ducked into the entrance of Al Siq as if it had had enough for one day. The Rangers grabbed the guide and scolded Billy in Arabic for wandering off during the downpour.

Billy sat on a rock and ignored them. He pulled off his boots and poured out the water. *I'll have to dry them slowly so the leather doesn't stretch,* thought Billy more concerned with his boots than the cuts and bruises on his head and arms. Without warning the rain stopped as fast as it began. Billy laughed to himself and thought, *Who says god ain't got a sense of humor?*

FOUR

Thumbach Bierpalast was a typical German beer garden with long tables on a patio covered with a wooden arbor. The majority of patrons were off-duty U.S. soldiers. Turner and Lowell were seated at the end of a table catching up on the last seven years of scuttlebutt. A waitress brought two glass mugs filled with Helles - a malty pale lager from Bavaria. "So 3rd Armor's getting in a little target practice?" said Lowell.

"Officially, yes," said Turner. "Unofficially, we're just letting the Russians know we haven't forgotten them and we've still got a very mean bite."

"I hope they get the message. Hate to get in a war a year before my retirement."

"Yeah, about that... You've got twenty years in now, don't ya?"

"Twenty-one."

"You're an E-6. I thought the cutoff was twenty years active duty?"

"It was. It is. I got a waiver. Just before my retirement date, DARPA requested me for a special assignment. Field testing some equipment they've been developing. I got a two-year extension waiver on my enlistment. Good thing too. I didn't know what the hell I was gonna do after retirement. Ranching business ain't what it used to be."

"Lucky break?"

"Very lucky."

"Always gotta have a plan B," said Turner.

"I'm working on it, but the military's all I've known my entire adult life," said Lowell. "Hard to just switch gears and do something else."

"Amen to that."

"Only thing I'm qualified to do is to kill people."

"And you're good at it."

"Tell that to my career counselor."

"How about getting a job with a defense contractor? They're always looking for ex-army to fill their ranks."

"Those guys wanna see a college diploma in engineering or computer science. I barely got my G.E.D."

"What about security work?"

"You mean like mercenary shit?"

"Yeah, among other things."

"I don't know. I got into the army to fight for America. Fighting for someone else just doesn't feel right," said Lowell.

"Gotta do something."

"Yeah, I know. I'll figure something out sooner or later. Probably later," said Lowell. "Wait a minute... Master Sergeant makes you an E-8 and you got thirty years in. You gotta be coming up on retirement too, aren't ya?"

"I still have a year and a half, but yeah... It's coming up."

"So, what's your plan?"

"I was thinking about running for sheriff in my hometown."

"You a sheriff. Really?"

"I always believed you should be on one side of the law or the other."

"I think the other side's a bit more profitable," said Lowell. "Although Sheriff Turner does kinda has a ring to it."

"It do, don't it?" said Turner with a smile.

"It's been a long journey, since Iraq," said Lowell. "If it wasn't for you watching out for me and teaching me how not to get killed, I probably wouldn't be here."

"Probably not. You were really stupid."

Both men laughed.

"But I'll be damned if you couldn't shoot the wings off a gnat. In a battle, sometimes that's all that matters."

"Damn right," said Lowell.

"Corporal Nelson sure couldn't shoot straight," said Turner.

"No. He couldn't."

"Piss poor excuse for a soldier," said Turner. "Whatever happened to him?"

"After you got transferred to 3rd Armor, they made me team commander. We were loading the tanks with supplies and this Iraqi patrol comes up over a hill and opens fire. Corporal Nelson was the only one with a rifle, so he returns fire while we hit the dirt. Damned if he didn't empty his clip without ever hitting a god damn thing. Towelheads shot him through the neck."

"What did you do?"

"Picked up his rifle, reloaded and opened fire while the medic tended to Nelson. He died before we could get him to a field hospital."

"That's too bad about Nelson," said Turner. "You hit any of 'em? The towelheads?"

"Yeah. Those that stayed and fought. The rest hauled ass back to Baghdad or some other place. Nelson may not have been much of a shot, but at least he stood his ground when it mattered most. Probably saved our lives."

"To the fallen," said Turner as he raised his glass.

"To the fallen," said Lowell, raising his glass. "And to standing your ground when it counts."

"To standing your ground," said Turner.

The two warriors drank in silence.

Billy sat alone in a Jordanian hotel lounge in an oversized chair nursing his wounds with two-fingers of Jack Daniel over ice. The wooden chair he sat in was a work of art with detailed carvings in the apron, rails, and legs. Colorful woven cushions padded the seat and back. His father was an amateur carpenter and had taught Billy to appreciate a handcrafted chair like this one. While growing up, Billy had helped his father make all the furniture in their house and learned how to make repairs to the barn and stables on their horse ranch. The old arts were of little use in a modern world of disposable everything, but Billy didn't care. He liked the chair in which he sat and he didn't much care what others did or thought.

He liked the hotel lounge too. It was a bit fancy for his taste, but it reminded him of the Riad he stayed at in Morocco. Like a traditional Riad, the lounge was the center court in the structure with tall pillars supporting the walls that formed an inner vestibule. The ceiling towered four-stories above and had large glass panes forming geometric Islamic patterns. A weighty brass and ceramic lamp hung down from a chain in the center and lit the room like a fire illuminating a cave. The floor was inlaid with small ceramic tiles that also formed geometric patterns – an Islamic custom. It was more than a bar or lobby. It was a gathering place for friends and family filled with couches and chairs arranged in groups, like individual living rooms without walls. A place to converse about the news of the day or a place to just sit alone and enjoy two-fingers of Jack.

A band of three musicians played time-honored Arab music softly in the corner of the lounge. The oud was played like a guitar, the reed pipe and the drum - simple and rhythmic. As his glass of the amber liquid emptied, Billy's eyes closed and he was carried away to a far-off land... home... Wyoming...

The grass was long and tan in the late summer. The chiseled mountain peaks still had patches of snow and the sky was as blue as a sapphire. The rivers ran shallow and slow.

Two teenager brothers, Billy and Lowell Gamble, ran their horses across a meadow at the edge of a mountain. As usual, Lowell had given Billy a five-second head start in the two-mile race. Only seventeen months apart in age, the boys were close in size, but Lowell's muscles were more defined and his face leaner having lost most of his baby fat long ago. At fifteen, Billy still had his boyish looks. He was cute and it pissed him off to no end when people mentioned it. Lowell was becoming a man and Billy was still stuck in childhood. None of this mattered when they were racing. Billy had the advantage because he was lighter in the saddle, but Lowell was willing to push his mount harder, especially if the race was close. Lowell hated to lose. Billy did too, but he had gotten used to it. Their family ranch was located well out of town and the distance made it difficult to visit friends. The brothers were their own best friends and worst enemies. Competitions were fierce and frequent. "Come on, Snowdrop," said Billy, standing in his stirrups as the horse ran. "You can do it."

Billy's horse pushed ahead a few feet, increasing his lead. "That-a-boy," said Billy. "Kick his ass."

Lowell's face soured and he became more determined. He used the ends of his reins as a whip, smacking the horse on both sides of its shoulders. "Move your butthole, Little Joe," said Lowell giving the reins an extra hard crack.

At the end of the meadow, the boys charged over a hilltop and down a slope to the river's edge. The horses hit the water with a splash drenching both riders. The river was deep in the middle, and the horses were forced to swim. Lowell slipped off his saddle and let himself float. His horse picked up speed and passed Billy's horse straining to swim with a full load. "That ain't fair, Lowell," said Billy.

"Don't be a pussy, Billy," said Lowell slipping back into the saddle as his horse found its footing on the opposite side of the river.

It was Lowell that had the lead as the two horse charged out of the river and up the embankment.

Lowell and Billy jumped off their horses inside the barn. They attached hitching post ropes to the rings on the horses' halters. The horses were steamy from sweat with a white lather built up around their cinches and breast straps. "We should've cooled 'em down more 'fore we came back to the barn," said Billy.

"Nah. We'll just brush 'em real good and throw their blankets on so they don't catch a cold. They'll be fine," said Lowell.

Billy pulled out his last piece of bubblegum from his jeans pocket, unwrapped it, and popped it into his mouth. He liked gum, especially when he started chewing a fresh piece and he got a rush of flavor.

"When you gonna give me the five bucks?" said Lowell.

"I ain't. You cheated," said Billy, chewing the gum.

"Ain't no rule says I have to stay in the saddle, you puss-wad."

"Bullshit, Lowell. It ain't a horse race if you ain't got no rider."

"Don't be a welcher, Billy. You lost. Pay up."

"I ain't paying you jack-shit, Lowell."

"Okay. You wanna play that way. Fine," said Lowell. "I'm telling Mary Lund you still wet the bed."

Billy's expression darkened. He had a crush on Mary Lund. "That's a lie and you know it," said Billy.

"Yeah, but she won't know it's a lie," said Lowell.

"If you do, Lowell, I'm gonna…"

"You ain't gonna do shit, you hairless turd," said Lowell. "Cuz you're a pussy and you always will be."

Lowell had crossed the invisible line. Billy knew he couldn't let it stand or he'd be living in fear forever. When Lowell reached up to hang up his horse's bit, Billy pulled the wad of bubblegum from his mouth and stuck it under Lowell's armpit tangling it in his pubescent hair. Billy knew Lowell was going to be mad. He just didn't know how mad. He probably should have thought more about it before placing the gum because Lowell was between the door and him. "What the fuck?" said Lowell staring at the gum in his armpit with a slight feeling of shock. "You're gonna die, you little piece of shit."

Billy believed him. Lowell was faster, stronger and much, much meaner than Billy and if he caught him Lowell would probably kill him. Billy ducked under Snowdrop preventing Lowell from grabbing him. He ran for the ladder leading to the hayloft and leapt onto the third rung. Lowell was right behind him and grabbed his left foot. Billy held on for dear life as Lowell pulled his leg, trying to pry him off the ladder. Billy was losing his grip. He kicked out with his right foot and hit Lowell squarely in the face with the heel of his boot. Lowell fell backward, his nose bleeding badly. Billy knew Lowell would be waiting outside when Billy crawled through the loft window and used the rope on the hay winch to let himself down to the ground. He would catch Billy and unleash hell. So, Billy did the only thing he could do... He jumped off the ladder and landed on top of Lowell laying on the floor. Billy landing on Lowell's chest knocked the air out of Lowell. Billy grabbed Lowell's right wrist and rolled off Lowell. Before Lowell could catch his breath, Billy twisted his arm behind his back and forced him to lay face down on the floor. Lowell tried to turn around. Billy wrenched his arm higher. Lowell groaned in pain. "Let go of me now and I won't kill you," said Lowell.

"I don't believe you," said Billy, starting to panic. This was the first time in Billy's young life he had ever gotten the better of his brother and it truly was unknown territory for him.

There was no way out for either of them. Billy couldn't let Lowell up and Lowell couldn't break free of Billy's arm-lock. "DAD!" shouted Billy toward the house.

Billy knew there was little hope of his father hearing him, but he had to do something... anything. "All right, shit-for-brains," said Lowell. "I gave you a chance to live. Now, I'm coming for you."

"No, Lowell. Don't."

"Too late, ass-wipe," said Lowell as he struggled to his knees, raising Billy up on his back. "I'm gonna break you in two and feed you to the hogs."

Billy panicked and pushed up on Lowell's arm with everything he had in hopes of forcing him back down. There was a loud crack and Lowell fell back to the floor screaming in pain. Billy looked down at Lowell's arm. His eyes went wide on seeing the end of a broken bone sticking through Lowell's forearm.

Billy woke up in a cold sweat, still sitting in the oversized chair in the hotel lounge. A Jordanian waiter stood over him, gently shaking him awake. "Sorry," said Billy to the waiter. "Must've dozed off."

"You were dreaming," said the waiter handing him his bar bill.

Billy paid it and went off to his room.

FIVE

A well-dressed executive with a briefcase walked into an office building in Belgium. He showed his badge to the guard at the security station; it read 'Gustaaf Visser.' He placed his briefcase on the conveyor belt for x-ray and walked through the metal detector. No beeps. A technician examined the briefcase as it passed through the x-ray system. His monitor showed there was something with wires inside the briefcase. He signaled to a second guard to check the briefcase. The guard asked Visser to open his briefcase. Visser opened it and the guard looked at the contents. A telephone headset. The guard picked it up and examined it. Nothing unusual. He placed it back inside the briefcase and told Visser he could close the briefcase and was free to enter the building.

Visser walked to the elevators and pressed the up button. Several other office workers joined him while waiting for the elevator. The elevator doors opened. The office workers and Visser stepped in, each pressing the button for their respective floors. Visser said 'Hello' in Dutch to familiar faces that entered the elevator. He pressed the button for the top floor and rode up with the others. The last person exited the elevator and the door closed. Visser was alone. He pressed the top floor button again, canceling his selection, then pressed the button for the basement. It was morning so the elevator went straight down without stopping.

When the door opened, Visser exited the elevator into the basement. He pulled out a schematic from his jacket and walked through a maze of pipes, cooling ducts, doorways and electrical panels using the schematic as a guide. He stopped in front of a doorway marked, 'Communications' and entered.

Moving to a panel in the small room marked 'Telephone System', he opened the panel's access door. Next, he opened his briefcase and removed the telephone headset with two alligator clips connected on the end of wires. He found the circuit marked 'maintenance' and clipped the alligator clips to the terminals, then to the metal rings on the plug-in connector on the headset. He tested the headset to see that it operated correctly. Satisfied, he set the headset down and exited the room.

Using the schematic as a guide, he made his way further into the basement and stopped in front of a series of valves. He looked at his schematic again to identify the valve he was searching for, before twisting the handle clockwise until it would not rotate further.

Inside a bathroom on the upper floors of the building, a woman exited a toilet stall and walked to the sink. She twisted the faucet handle. A small amount of water trickled out, then stopped completely. Frustrated, she cursed and stomped out of the bathroom to call building maintenance.

In the basement, Visser, now back in the communication room, listened on the headset as the women called in and complained to maintenance. He remained silent as the call was terminated. He waited. A light blinked on the headset. He pressed the connect button and answered the call. He spoke in Dutch as if he was the operator at the City's Water Department. He put the call on hold, waited a moment, then used a different voice to answer when he took the call off hold. He listened to the maintenance manager complain, then replied that he would send a team out ASAP to look into the problem. He hung up, removed the headset, and pulled out his mobile phone. "Go," he said into his phone and hung up. He exited the basement.

A few moments later, a man dressed as a City Water Department repairman exited his van, carrying his tool chest. He walked into the building and approached the security station.

The maintenance manager exited the elevator and approached the repairman. They spoke in Dutch. "That was fast," said the maintenance manager.

"You're lucky," said the repairman. "I was just down the street. Usually takes a few hours to get someone to respond. What's the problem?"

"Water's stopped."

The repairman grunted, "I'll take look. Where's the elevator?"

"Over there," the manager said pointing. "You want me to go down with you?"

"Nah. I can handle it. Troubleshooting can take a while and I'm sure you've got better things to do. I'll call your office once I figure out the problem."

"Thanks," said the manager.

The repairman moved off to the elevator with his tool chest.

The maintenance manager sat at this desk filling out a requisition form. The repairman appeared in the doorway and knocked before entering. "So, what did you find?" said the manager.

"It's not good. Looks like you got a leak in the flange between the building's main line and the city's street line. We're gonna have to replace it. I'm gonna need a set of blueprints for the building, so we know where to cut."

"Cut? Cut what?"

"We've got to cut a hole in the basement northern wall to get access to the street main, otherwise we've got to enter through the street and that could take a month just to get the permit."

"Jesus. How long is this going to take?"

"Assuming I can get a crew out right away and that the replacement junction is in stock... could take a week, maybe ten days."

"Without water?" said the manager, alarmed.

"It's a downtown street main. They're big. It takes time."

"What about the toilets?"

"They can still flush the toilets. Just keep a pail of water by each bowl and they can toss it in when they're finished with their business."

"The tenants are going have my ass."

"Yeah. That's why I stay out of management. Too much stress," said the repairman. "Well, I'd better get to it. I'll have the replacement junction delivered to your loading dock as soon as it arrives from our supply warehouse... assuming that it's in stock."

"Yeah," said the manager weakly, his career flashing before his eyes.

The repairman left the building.

SIX

Lowell sat munching on a Snickers bar as several Army technicians worked on Thunder. "Sergeant, can ya fire her up and test the minigun?" said the lead technician, Specialist Cox.

Cox knew more about Thunder than almost anyone. He had spent countless hours in the weapon system simulator learning the drone's intricacies. He never understood why the Army commander in charge of weapons procurement had chosen Staff Sergeant Gamble over him for the field tests. It didn't make sense. The sergeant was an old warhorse. Cox was a young stallion and knew far more about the computers that controlled Thunder. He was absolutely positive that in a heads-up match in a military multiplayer game like Call of Duty or Battlefield, he would kick Staff Sergeant Gamble's ass up one side and down the other.

"Sure thing," said Lowell as he moved into the control cockpit container, entered the access code into the weapon system keyboard. The video monitors and control panels came to life and Lowell slipped on the headset. He used the joystick to focus in on a distant Humvee traveling across the base. Thunder's auto-targeting system locked on the Humvee. "Thunder, engage minigun," said Lowell in his headset.

Outside the container, a panel opened on the drone and Thunder's minigun rose up and swung around toward the Humvee. The M134 minigun was capable of firing two thousand 7.65mm rounds per minute and was used to attack soft targets like infantry, trucks, and jeeps. "Minigun up," said Thunder over the headset.

Lowell squeezed the trigger on the joystick.

Cox watched as the minigun's six barrels rotated with a high-speed whirr but didn't fire. It was not loaded. "Minigun ammunition empty," said Thunder over the headset.

"All right, kill it, Sergeant," said Cox, satisfied that the system was working properly.

Lowell released the trigger. "Thunder, ceasefire minigun," said Lowell.

The minigun lowered back into Thunder's body and the panel closed.

Lowell re-entered the access code and shut down the control cockpit.

Garza approached as Lowell exited the control cockpit container. He snapped to and saluted her along with the technicians. "At ease," said Garza. "Sergeant, is your team gonna be packed up and ready for an on-time departure?"

"Yes, Ma'am. If the river don't rise," said Lowell.

"What the hell is that supposed to mean? We gonna make it or not?"

"We'll make it, Ma'am."

"Good. See to it. I want to stay on schedule."

"Roger that, Ma'am," said Lowell saluting Garza. He couldn't help but glance at her tight ass as she moved off. Lowell knew it was against U.S. Army policy for an enlisted soldier like himself to carry on a romantic relationship with an officer in the same unit, but he figured it was more the Lieutenant's problem than his if someone found out and squealed on them. She was, after all, his superior officer… and an animal in the sack.

The crew of technicians packed up their tools and test equipment. Thunder moved toward the back of the control cockpit container. It was a convenient and compact package – the control cockpit and drone storage facility in one shipping container. It made it easier to guard and allowed for minimal personnel.

Lowell sat in the control cockpit and maneuvered Thunder through the open doors into the back half of the container. Once Thunder was inside, Lowell again shut down the control room and exited the container.

The technicians closed and locked the heavy metal doors on the rear of the container. Thunder was secured and ready for transport.

A winch with cable pulled the control cockpit and storage container onto the back of an M1000 semi-trailer pulled by a U.S. Army M1070 tractor truck, the same combination designed to transport the M1A Abrams tank weighing sixty tons. It was complete overkill. Even with the control cockpit and anti-tank drone combined, the Thunder weapon system weighed a fraction of the main battle tank. Thunder used speed, agility, and stealth over heavy armor. It could handle the punishment of small arms fire and even survive an RPG, but a sabot round from a modern battle tank would punch through its composite skin like a hot knife through butter. Still, the Army wasn't taking any chances with its new toy and assigned a Heavy Equipment Transport System to the Thunder project.

The technicians used turnbuckles to secure the container to the flatbed trailer. Thunder was ready for its journey to Ramstein Air Base in southwestern Germany where it would be loaded into a C-17 Globemaster III transport aircraft and flown back to America courtesy of the U.S. Air Force.

The concept of the new weapon system was simple. Thunder was cheap to manufacture and deploy when compared to the cost of an M1A Abrams tank, plus it was a drone, so there was no crew needed to put into harm's way. In a major conflict, the U.S. Army would hide hundreds of the anti-tank drones directly in the path of the advancing enemy. When the enemy passed, the anti-tank drones would attack from the rear, focusing on the destruction of their enemy's heavy armor. The bulk of the U.S. forces and its allies would then use their main battle tanks to attack from the front in a pincher movement like a scorpion's claw crushing the enemy. U.S. Air Power – the scorpion's tail – would finish off any remaining enemy units. Simple, sneaky, and effective… just the way the U.S. war planners liked it.

Lowell always rode in the passenger seat of the truck pulling the trailer. Thunder was his responsibility while it was overseas. Only he knew the access code that unlocked the drone. Until field testing was completed that's the way the wonks at DARPA wanted it - limited access with one-man control. There were too many things to screw up on an advanced weapons system for more than one operator at a time. And if something got damaged they knew who to blame.

Lowell was chosen for the project because of his combat experience and the scores on his entry test when he joined the military. He may have played the part of a rough and tumble cowboy from Wyoming, but Lowell was smart and a workhorse that could handle the long hours the job required without complaint. When first assigned to the program, he had stayed up all night reading the weapon system manuals and learned to operate Thunder in just a few days. The wonks were impressed. Of course, there were other soldiers that learned the weapon system, including the small army of technicians that accompanied it, but it was Lowell that was given the keys to the kingdom – the access code.

Lowell stayed close to the drone as much as possible. And when he wasn't around, the attachment of MPs protected Thunder. Garza and the MP's rode in five Humvees, three of which were armed with .50-cal machine guns mounted on rooftop turrets. Three troop trucks carried the technicians, their equipment and spare parts for the weapon system.

Lowell prepared to board the truck. Garza approached. "Sergeant, I'm gonna need another debriefing once we reach Ramstein Air Base and unload the gear," said Garza.

"Roger that, Lieutenant," said Lowell. "I'll keep it short and sweet."

"No need for that. Just make sure you're thorough," said Garza. "It's gonna be a long flight back to America."

Lowell cracked a slight smile. Esposito approached and said, "L.T., we've got a problem."

"What's that, Sergeant?"

"Specialist Cox just informed me one of his technicians forgot some of his equipment back in the barracks."

"Shit," said Garza looking at her watch. "All right, Sergeant. Take a couple of guys and the backup deuce and a half. Go fetch whatever he left behind. I don't want to get off schedule, so we're gonna go ahead and hit the road. You can catch up."

"Roger that, Ma'am," said Esposito and moved off.

"Let's get this show on the road," said Garza. The rest of the MP's and technicians boarded their trucks and Humvees. The convoy with the semi-truck pulling the Thunder weapon system in the middle pulled out and headed for the main gate. Specialist Cox and two of the MP's joined Esposito in the backup truck and drove off in the opposite direction.

The convoy carrying Thunder moved through the main gate at the front of the base. Garza road in the passenger seat of the second Humvee in front of Lowell in the semi-cab and trailer.

Esposito, Cox and the two MPs pulled up in front of the base armory in the two and a half ton truck. They entered the concrete building through a doorway.

Inside the armory, they approached the front desk where a corporal sat at a desk. "Afternoon, Sergeant. What can I do for you?" said the corporal.

"Got a list of supplies I need to pick up," said Esposito handing the corporal the list.

"Wow. You guys starting a war?" said the corporal with a chuckle until he saw that Esposito was unamused. "Okay. No problem. You got a signed requisition?"

"Nope. No time for paperwork," said Esposito.

"I can't give you anything without the proper paperwork, Sergeant. Quartermaster would have my ass."

Esposito pulled out his sidearm, chambered a round and pointed the pistol at the corporal's face. "I'm gonna need you to make an exception just this once. You understand, don't ya, Corporal?"

The corporal nodded.

"Good of you to be so cooperative, Corporal. Now fetch us everything on that list toot-sweet before I get ornery and put a bullet in your ass."

"I'm gonna need the forklift for some of this stuff," said the corporal. "It's in the back."

Esposito nodded to Cox.

"I'll get it," said Cox and he moved off toward the back of the armory.

The corporal moved into shelves of the armory followed by Esposito and the MPs. The corporal stopped in front a stack of thirty ammunition tubes strapped together on a wooden palette. Each tube was labeled, "1-Cartridge, 120mm APFSDS" and had a unique serial number. "These are the sabots. Thirty to a palette," said the corporal. "You guys know it's a felony to take one of these shells off base?"

"Shut the fuck up, Corporal, and show us where we can find the HEAT rounds," said Esposito as Cox rolled up with the forklift, lifted one of the palettes and drove off toward the front of the building.

Outside the armory, the roll-up door opened and the forklift rolled out and over to the truck. Cox loaded the Sabot rounds into the back, then drove back into the armory to pick up more ammunition and equipment.

The sergeant inspected the completed bridge his platoon of engineers had built. He checked the bolts to ensure they were secure and bounced up and down on the boards that formed the driving surface to ensure there were no loose boards. "Good work, soldiers," said the sergeant. "Now blow the damn thing up."

The engineers took great pride in their finished bridge, but blowing shit up was just plain fun and why most of them became engineers in the first place. It was unlikely that many of them would ever see action in a war, but they loved to practice.

The engineers moved from the riverbank to a truck parked on the road. They opened up the back flap and pulled out several crates of explosives, spools of detcord and fuses. The sergeant glanced at the back of the truck and snarled, "What the holy hell is that?"

"What, Sergeant?" said Corporal Wright standing next to him.

"I told you to pick up enough explosive to blow the bridge."

"Yes, Sergeant."

"Corporal, you've got enough C-4 to blow up the Kremlin and everything else in Red Square."

"Yes, Sergeant. I didn't want to run short."

"Run short?"

Corporal Wright hit the sergeant over the back of the head with a shovel, knocking him out. He crumpled to the ground unconscious. Wright motioned to three other engineers in the platoon. They closed up the back and climbed into the truck. Wright climbed into the cab and drove off leaving the other members of the platoon to wonder why the corporal had beaned their sergeant on the head.

The trucks filled with the weapons and ammunition from the armory moved toward the main gate at the base. The truck carrying the engineers and the explosives pulled in behind it and followed. The main gate MPs had not yet been notified of either incident and waved the mini-convoy through. It was business as usual.

SEVEN

The convoy carrying Thunder was making good time moving through the German countryside. The yellow, orange and red hues of the leaves still on the trees and the quaint villages made the drive pleasant. Passengers stared out at the military vehicles as a high-speed bullet train sped past the convoy. The American troops which had been vanquished for many years were once again a welcome novelty as things heated up between the East and West. Russia was again on the rise and the Germans weren't taking any chances. The East Germans especially had no desire to return to a life under Russia's thumb. Capitalism had been harsh in many respects, but the freedom to do and say what you wished was a worthwhile tradeoff.

The German civilians around the U.S. Army base were used to seeing military convoys and tended to pull over to get out of the way. It was safer. The Army trucks and Humvees were massive compared to most German cars and trucks.

Lowell kept the passenger door window down even though the autumn air was brisk. It kept him awake and alert. It also reminded him of Wyoming in the fall when he and his brother Billy would put up the alfalfa bales in the barn's loft. The first snow would usually arrive in early November and the horses their family raised and trained would need plenty of forage to make it through a Wyoming winter. It was hard work. The bales were heavy. The boys would both sweat until their shirts were damp with perspiration. The cool autumn breeze was always welcome.

Lowell was surprised when he saw the Humvee Garza was riding in pull over to the side of the road. "Where in the hell is she going?" said Lowell.

"I suppose even Lieutenants have to pee sometimes," said the technician driving. "Should I pull over?"

"No," said Lowell. "Not unless she gives us orders. They can catch up."

Lowell watched out the window as the truck and trailer drove past the Humvee. He was riding too high to see anything inside the Humvee. He watched in the rearview mirror as the convoy moved on. He saw the three MPs riding with the Lieutenant get out and move to the passenger door. They opened the door and pulled Garza out of the vehicle. They punched her, then kicked her as she fell to the ground. "What the fuck?" said Lowell sticking his head out the window and looking back. "Pull over!"

The tractor and trailer pulled off to the side of the road. As the truck slowed, Lowell reached for the door handle. "Can't let you leave, Sergeant," said the Technician. "I've got my orders."

Lowell turned to see the Technician pointing a pistol at Lowell. "Just relax, Sergeant," said the Technician. "Nobody needs to get hurt."

"What the fuck is going on?" said Lowell.

"We're stealing Thunder," said the Technician.

The truck was still rolling to a stop when Lowell reach over and grabbed the Technician's wrist holding the pistol.

"The hell you are," he said.

He lifted the Technician's arm toward the ceiling and the pistol fired a round into the cab's padded headliner and through the roof. Lowell punched the

Technician in the face three times, very hard and very fast, knocking him unconscious. His pistol fell from his limp hand on the cab's floor. Lowell opened the driver's side door and pushed the technician out of the cab onto the road.

A Humvee pulling up alongside the truck's cab had to slam on its brakes to avoid running over the technician.

Lowell slid into the driver's seat and slammed the door shut. He hit the brakes hard and the truck skidded to a stop. Lowell slammed the gearshift into reverse and hit the gas as he watched the rearview mirror and the trailer's backup camera monitor. He could see the three MPs continuing to hit and kick Garza. The truck lurched as it started to move in reverse.

The MP driving the Humvee behind the trailer looked up at the back of the trailer headed straight for his vehicle. He slammed on his brakes and threw his gearshift into reverse. Too late. The back of the trailer smashed into the front of the Humvee and pushed it backward. The driver pulled up the handle of his emergency brake and locked the Humvee's wheels. It slowed the truck and trailer but didn't stop it. The Humvee's wheels skidded leaving black rubber across the pavement. The back of the Humvee slammed into the front of a second Humvee and pushed it backward. The truck and trailer were slowing from the additional friction.

Lowell punched the pedal to the floor and the engine roared.

The truck's wheels spun backward, bouncing off the pavement. The truck kept moving backward, pushing the two Humvees with it. The two trucks holding the technicians swerved out of the way and off the road. Lowell stopped the truck as it pulled up parallel with Garza's Humvee. He picked up the pistol the technician had dropped in the cab, jumped out and ran over to the MPs punching and kicking Garza. He leveled the pistol, "Knock it off or you're dead men," shouted Lowell.

They stopped. Garza looked up, her face bloodied. She smiled at Lowell. A pistol whipped across the back of Lowell's head. He crumpled to the ground, unconscious. Esposito stepped from behind and looked down at Lowell. "Bring him," he said to the MPs.

Lowell woke up when a bucket of cold water hit him in the face. He looked around, groggy, at what looked like the interior of a meat packing plant. There were hooks hanging from overhead racks and a band saw for cutting sides of beef or pork in half. The place smelled of putrid animal flesh. His wrists and ankles were tied to a chair with plastic ties. Esposito was standing across a wooden table. He was sharpening the blade on his K-bar knife using a butcher's steel that he had found. "We don't have much time, Sergeant," said Esposito. "Give me the access code to Thunder."

"Fuck off, you traitor," said Lowell.

"Good. Right to the point," said Esposito. "I like that. No sense in wasting time on meaningless chit-chat. We both know where this is going. So let's get to it."

"Knock it off, Sergeant Esposito," said a voice Lowell recognized.

Esposito stepped to one side revealing Turner approaching the table. "Master Sergeant?" said Lowell, confused.

"Hey, Lowell," said Turner. "Sorry about all this."

"What the hell is going on?"

"This is your new plan B if you want it. Just give us the access code and you can join us. You'll be set for life. Buy your own island kinda set."

"Stealing Thunder is treason."

"Maybe. At least that's the way the provost marshal will probably see it if we're caught. But we ain't gonna get caught, Lowell. It took years, but everything has been planned to the last detail. All we need to do now is execute and to do that we need the code."

Lowell's head was spinning. He wasn't sure if it was the concussion he was fairly sure he had or just the unbelievable truth unfolding before him. "It was you that arranged for my enlistment extension with DARPA?" said Lowell.

"They asked for my recommendation and I gave them your name."

"Why?"

"I can trust you. Beneath that shit-kicking cowboy demeanor is a real thinker. Someone that can see a once-in-a-lifetime opportunity and is ambitious enough to grab it. Think of what it will mean to you and your family to never worry again. You've paid your dues to your country. Now it's time to pay yourself. You're gonna be rich, Lowell. I promise."

"You expect me to take you at your word?"

"Yes. We fought together. That's a bond that can't be easily broken and you know it."

"I never thought it could... until now. You overestimate me. I'm not that smart. You can pound sand before I give you the access code to Thunder."

"Don't do this, Staff Sergeant."

"It's already done, Master Sergeant. I made up my mind long ago. I'll die before I betray my country. Like Esposito said... let's get to it."

"That is a shame," said Turner turning to Esposito. "Be quick, Sergeant. We have a schedule to keep"

"Roger that," said Esposito stepping forward and slipping his newly sharpened K-bar back into its sheath.

Esposito moved to Lowell's side and knelt down. He placed the butcher's steel into the plastic tie holding Lowell's hand to the chair. He twisted it like a tourniquet. The plastic strap cut into Lowell's wrist until it snapped. Lowell's hand was free. Lowell squeezed his hand into a fist to get the blood flowing again, then set it down on the table. His wrist was bleeding from the cut. Esposito swung the blunt point of the butcher's steel down through the center of Lowell's hand and into the wood table top. Lowell screamed. "God, that's gotta hurt. Have I got your attention, Staff Sergeant? Cuz I am going to need it for this next part," said Esposito as he pulled out his K-bar knife.

"You're wasting time, Sergeant Esposito. I know the man. You can carve him up all day and he ain't gonna tell you squat," said Turner.

"I don't know about that, Master Sergeant."

"I do," said Turner. "Let's move things along."

"Yes, Master Sergeant," said Esposito nodding to Specialist Cox standing by the door.

Cox went into the next room and brought Garza back out, her hands bound with a plastic tie. "You're all going to fucking hang," said Garza.

"Show some style, L.T.," said Cox. "Don't make me tape your big mouth shut."

Cox lifted Garza up while Esposito threaded a meat hook through the plastic tie that cuffed her hands together and hung her from an overhead rack like a side of beef. Esposito used his newly sharpened K-bar to cut the buttons off her uniform's blouse. The blouse opened exposing her bra. "Nice, L.T.," said Esposito admiring her breasts.

"Don't you give the code, Lowell," said Garza.

"Brave," said Esposito. "I admire that in an officer."

"Fuck you, Esposito," said Garza.

"Well if you had, Lieutenant, you probably wouldn't be here. Instead, you fucked him," said Esposito pointing to Lowell. "Bad move."

"I'm gonna kill you, Esposito," said Lowell.

Esposito walked over and grabbed the handle of the butcher's steel and gave it a shake. Lowell winced in pain. "Really, Sergeant?" said Esposito. "Is that what's happening here? You're gonna kill me? Cuz it doesn't look like that from where I'm standing. What is going to happen… is I'm gonna start skinning the Lieutenant starting with her beautiful breasts. You feel free to jump in at any time with that access code and I'll stop. Deal?"

Esposito walked over to Garza, placed the blade of his K-bar above her left breast and made a long shallow slice. Garza screamed. "All right," said Lowell. "Enough."

"That was quick," said Esposito. "You were right, Master Sergeant. "Love does trump pain."

"Shut up, Esposito," said Turner. "The code, Staff Sergeant?"

Inside the control cockpit half of the shipping container, a technician sat in the chair and keyed in the access code as he listened over the headset. The video monitors and control panel blinked on. He typed in a command and the auto-targeting system turned on. "We're in business," said the technician over the headset.

Inside the meat packing plant, Esposito smiled. "That was a lot easier than I thought it was going to be."

"Sergeant Esposito, if you don't shut up, I'm gonna put my fist in your mouth and pull your tongue out," said Turner.

Turner approached Cox and said, "Get the L.T. down and everyone loaded up. I want to move in three minutes."

"Roger that, Master Sergeant," said Cox.

"What shall we do with him?" said Esposito motioning to Lowell.

"Don't be dense, Sergeant," said Turner turning to Lowell. "It didn't need to be this way, Lowell."

"Fuck you," said Lowell.

Turner pulled out his pistol and shot Lowell in the chest. Lowell gasped for air, blood sputtered from his mouth and he slumped over, motionless. "Make sure nobody finds his body," said Turner to two MPs – Private Miller and Corporal Butler. "We'll leave you a Humvee."

"Copy that, Master Sergeant," said Butler as Esposito and Cox gently lowered Garza and carried her out.

Outside the building, the team mounted up and drove away leaving a Humvee.

Inside the meat packing plant, Miller pulled out his K-bar and cut Lowell's hand and feet lose from the chair. He set his knife down on the table and gripped the handle on the butcher's steel with both hands and pulled. It didn't budge. "Damn it," said Miller to himself.

Butler reentered the room and said, "I found a commercial hamburger grinder in the next room. Probably be faster to grind him up rather than bury him."

Lowell raised his head. His free hand picked up the knife from the table and plunged the blade deep into Miller's chest just above his sternum. Miller fell to the floor and died. Butler was shocked to see Lowell still alive and on the attack. "Oh shit," said Butler as he reached for his sidearm.

Lowell stood up and struggled for breath, coughing up blood as he grabbed the handle of the butcher's steel and yanked it out of the table with his good hand. He threw the steel like a dagger across the room and into Butler's left eye with such force the blunt tip of the rod went all the through and popped out the back of the man's head. Butler dropped his gun, collapsed and died.

Lowell felt tired. He sat back down in the chair and his chest heaved as he tried to catch his breath. He coughed out blood until he could breathe again.

He could hear the air sucking through the bullet hole. *Sucking chest wound. That's bad,* he thought. He rose and walked over to Miller's body, removed his WEB belt with its holstered sidearm and attached it around his own waist. He searched Miller's pockets and pulled out a piece of paper with a list of numbers and letters. He stuffed the list into his own pocket. Then he walked over to Butler's body, picked up his pistol, tucked into his belt and searched Butler's pockets. He found another list and a 6-inch clear plastic ruler. He threw the ruler aside and stuffed the list in his pocket. He exited through the doorway.

Lowell stumbled out of the building. The convoy was nowhere in sight, but he saw the Humvee left behind for the MPs. He climbed into the Humvee and looked for the vehicle's radio. It had been removed and there was no way to call for help. He could barely breathe and felt exhausted. The air in his chest cavity prevented his lungs from expanding. He was also bleeding badly. He knew he was going to bleed-out and die before he could get any help. He leaned back in the seat. It felt good to sit. He was weak. The only thing keeping him awake was the pain. He knew if he passed out he probably wouldn't wake up. He pulled himself up and out of the seat, went to the back of the Humvee and opened the hatch.

He found the vehicle's first aid kit and opened it. He tore open his shirt exposing the bullet wound. His hands were shaking. He sat down on the vehicle's bumper to steady himself. He opened a package of coagulant agent and dumped it directly into the chest wound and into the hole in his hand. It helped with the bleeding, but he still had a problem with air entering the chest wound. He opened a field dressing and a triangular bandage and set them aside on the lid of the first aid kit, so they wouldn't get dirty but were within reach. He opened a package of gauze and rolled it tight. He took as deep a breath as he could and steeled himself for the pain that he was about to inflict on himself. He pushed the tight roll of gauze down into the bullet hole in his chest using his little finger as a ramrod. The air entering his chest through the bullet hole stopped. He already had a lot of air in his chest cavity, but he hoped it would leak out and allow him to breathe easier in an hour or so. The bullet rattling around someplace inside him didn't scare him. He knew lots of guys with bullets inside their bodies and they functioned just fine. *The bullet has already done all the damage it's going to do and I'm still standing,* he thought. *Fuck it.* He placed the field dressing over the bullet hole and used the triangular bandage to wrap around his chest and keep the field dressing in place. He opened a second field dressing and placed it on his hand, then used an ace bandage to wrap around his hand to keep the dressing in place. It all looked sloppy like the work of a third-grader, but it served its purpose.

Lowell had stopped most of the bleeding and the air entering his chest. He leaned against the side of the hatch and took a moment to rest and clear his head. The moment was over all too soon. "Enough slacking, cowboy. Get your ass up and get a move on," he said to himself.

He closed the hatch and moved to the driver's seat. It felt good to sit again. Even the smallest movement seemed to require an immense amount of effort. He grabbed the steering wheel and squeezed with his wounded hand. The pain snapped him from his malaise. "Knock it off, you pussy," he said to himself as he started the engine and sped off in pursuit of the convoy.

The Humvee drove up to an intersection of main roads and pulled to a stop. Lowell looked out through the windshield. There were three directions they could have gone and no indication which road they took. There was an MGSR map book sitting on the passenger seat. He flipped it open. Several pages were torn out of the book. He turned to the page where he was currently located based on the street signs. He had hoped there would be some pencil scribbles or markings to indicate the direction they may have taken. There were none. He looked for the closest highway figuring that was a good of a guess as any. He cranked the wheel and drove off in the direction of the highway.

EIGHT

Back on the base, Lieutenant Tien sat at a desk finishing her paperwork on the drug-theft bust. There was still a lot that needed to be done to ensure that the U.S. Army prosecutor was successful in convicting the two servicemen that she had arrested. The fate of the two servicemen would be determined by court-martial using the uniform military code of justice. As the investigator and the arresting officer, she knew she would be called as a witness. She was articulate, straightforward and came off as honest. She made a good witness and her cases had a high conviction rate. She guessed the two soldiers would spend ten to twelve years in a military prison before they were released with dishonorable discharges.

There was also the hospital janitor that would need to be prosecuted. He was a civilian and would need to be put on trial in a civil court where the burden of proof was higher and a jury of his peers would decide his fate. She would dot every "I" and cross every "T" to ensure that nobody got off on her watch. Tien was nothing if not detailed and thorough. They had messed with the wrong MP... even if they didn't know it at the time.

She knew she was going to catch all sorts of hell for shooting a suspect in handcuffs, even though she had warned him. Putting pressure on his gunshot wound with her boot could very well have saved his life but gave the wrong impression. In hindsight, it was probably not the best idea. *I did what I had to do to get the job done,* she thought. *There was no shame in it.* Her rationalization would be of little help before a promotion board reviewing her record. Even though she was big for an American Vietnamese, most of the men she arrested were much larger than her and all were trained to fight and kill like herself. The Beretta M9 pistol that she always carried was the great equalizer and she wasn't afraid to use it. That was the problem. She used it a lot. Her job was to investigate serious felonies. The suspects knew if arrested and convicted, they would spend a good portion if not all of their lives in Leavenworth, the U.S. Military's correction facility in Kansas. *If I want to make captain, I really got to stop shooting people,* she thought, determined to turn over a new leaf.

Tien could see Captain Tillman through the glass wall that enclosed his office. He was shaking his head and cursing to himself as he read a report on his desk. Something was obviously upsetting him and she hoped it wasn't her.

Tillman was the commander of the MPs on the U.S. Army base in Grafenwöhr, but he wasn't her commander. She was a CID special agent and reported up through an independent chain of command to the Provost Marshall General at the Pentagon. Tillman cooperated with her as ordered, but he didn't like it. He ran a tight ship and didn't like anything or anyone he couldn't control.

Tillman was like most MP commanders. Tien had learnt to put up with their dismissive attitudes. She needed the commander's MPs to back her up when she made her arrests. Besides, she wasn't looking for friends. Moving from one base to another, investigating serious crime, she had no time for relationships. That was the way she liked it. She was good at her job and that was enough.

Tillman's phone rang and he answered it. Tien couldn't hear the conversation, but she could see Tillman's mood darken even further as he listened. He hung up the phone and dialed another number, then waved her into his office.

She entered his office as he hung up the phone again. "What's up, Captain?"

"A shit storm, Lieutenant. That's what's up," said Tillman. "I've just been ordered to turn over this investigation to you. You should be receiving a call from your commanding officer shortly. There isn't a lot of time, so I will brief you now."

"Okay, sir," said Tien. She didn't like the irregularity of it, but she also knew this was not the best time to argue the point. Besides, she was curious and in most investigations the first two days were the most important. She didn't want to waste any time if it could be helped.

"Early this morning, the base armory was robbed. The new shift found the corporal in charge tied up in the storage closet."

"What'd they take?"

"Ammunition mostly. 120mm sabot and HEAT rounds."

"Tank shells?"

"Yeah. Plus some Mini Samson ROWS and other weapons."

"Holly shit," said Tien.

"My feelings exactly. But I'm just getting started," said Tillman. "A squad of engineers beaned their sergeant over the head and stole a truck filled with explosives. Then, one hour ago, twenty-one kilometers from the base, a rancher found two MPs dead with their sidearms missing. I've got a team on its way to the crime scene."

"I'm sorry for your loss, Captain," said Tien.

"Don't be. They weren't mine. They were part of a special detachment sent to protect an experimental DARPA weapon system here for field testing. The convoy carrying the DARPA project was on its way to Ramstein air base for a flight back to the U.S. Now, it's missing too."

"What kind of weapon system?"

"An anti-tank drone."

"Does it have a tracking system?"

"Yes. Thank god. That's about the only thing that hasn't gone wrong. The container carrying the weapon system is moving east like a bat out of hell. Looks like they're headed for the Polish border," said Tillman. "I've got a fire team of MPs, a Blackhawk and a Longbow gunship waiting for you at the airfield."

"We should inform the German police and have them set up roadblocks," said Tien.

"Why? We know where they're headed. I say we keep this thing as quiet as possible."

"Have you ever seen the damage a rogue tank can inflict on a civilian population?" said Tien.

"Can't say I have," said Tillman.

"Neither have I and I'd like to keep it that way," said Tien.

"You know the Germans are gonna be mighty pissed."

"I would imagine. But with all due respect, it's not your call, Captain."

"You're right. It ain't," said Tillman. "I'll call the Germans and make sure the roadblocks are set up. Good hunting, Lieutenant."

Tien saluted and exited, feeling the weight of the mountain of shit that was just dumped on her. She had been involved in a lot of investigations over the years, but nothing like this. This was the kind of thing that could make or break a career, not to mention cost a lot of people their lives.

Tien rode in the Blackhawk helicopter with a four-man fire team of MPs, three armed with M4 carbines and the fourth with a SAW machine gun. The

Blackhawk also had a door-gunner armed with a minigun mounted in the open doorway.

Trailing behind the Blackhawk was an Apache Longbow Gunship armed with a 30 mm M230 chain gun that was belly-mounted under it forward fuselage. The M230 chain gun could rip a standard Humvee in half in just under a second. And if that wasn't enough, the gunship had four Hydra rocket launchers, each housing 19-rocket tubes, mounted under the short wings on the sides of the fuselage. It was an impressive weapons platform. The Taliban nicknamed it 'The Monster' for good reason.

The two helicopters made good time and caught up with the tractor-trailer in a little over an hour. The Humvees and troop trucks were nowhere in sight. The Blackhawk swooped down beside the truck's cab. The driver ignored Tien's signals to pull over even when the Blackhawk's door gunner fired a stream of tracer bullets in front of the cab.

Tien radioed the gunship and ordered the pilot to stop the truck with force if necessary, but to avoid damaging the trailer and its precious cargo. The Apache flew ahead of the truck about a half mile and performed a high banking turn bringing it directly in front of the truck's cab. The helicopter's blades would slice into cab decapitating the driver should he elect to call the pilot's bluff. The pilot had no intention of letting his aircraft be harmed by the idiot driver and was prepared to pull up at the last second if necessary to avoid a collision. There were much easier and less dangerous methods of stopping the truck, such as firing a burst of 30 mm rounds into the radiator and engine block, but the pilot was a bit of a showboat like many Army pilots and liked the idea of an old-fashioned game of chicken. He was right. The truck driver slammed on the brakes and the truck skidded to a halt jackknifing the trailer across the road.

The Blackhawk swooped down and landed on the road behind the trailer cutting off any escape. Tien and her fire team poured out through the helicopter's doorway. Two of the MP's ran forward to the cab and pulled the driver out, slamming him on the ground. He was just a teenager wearing civilian clothes. Master Sergeant Turner had offered him 1000 Euros to drive the truck and trailer to the Polish border. The boy thought he was carrying a load of counterfeit Levi jeans.

Tien and the two other fire team members opened the doors of the trailer, keeping their weapons leveled at the ready. Thunder was gone and so was the equipment in the control cockpit.

NINE

It was night. Lowell woke up not knowing where he was. He could hear the Humvee's engine still running. The last thing he could remember was driving down a country road. He looked through the windshield and could see that the Humvee was in a ditch beside the road. He looked down at the bandage he had placed over his chest wound. It was soaked red. As near as he could figure, he had fainted from loss of blood and the Humvee had run off the road. He had gone as far as his body would allow. He was anemic and dehydrated. He knew he couldn't go to a hospital or even a doctor for fear of being reported. There was a plastic bottle of water that had rolled forward from underneath the passenger seat when the vehicle plowed into the ditch. He leaned over, picked up the bottle and drank. It hurt to drink, but he emptied the bottle anyway in hopes it would help his dehydration. His head cleared slightly. He threw the gearshift into reverse and backed the Humvee out of the ditch and back onto the road. He drove away.

Lowell parked the Humvee in front of a dark building with a sign in German reading, "Veterinary Clinic." Lowell couldn't read German, but the images of a dog, a cat and a bird on the sign reassured him that he had found the right place. He was weak and faint, his head reeling again. Lowell got out of the Humvee and moved to the back of the vehicle. He opened the back hatch and looked through the gear left by the MPs. He pulled out Miller's rucksack and emptied its contents in its main compartment – mostly civilian clothes and a plastic rain poncho. He didn't bother with the front or side pockets.

With the rucksack in hand, Lowell walked to the front door of the clinic. He picked up a hand-sized rock in the garden in the front of the building and hurled it into a floor-to-ceiling plate glass window. The glass shattered and he entered the building.

He moved through the hallway until he found the supply closet. Breaking the door open, he found the supplies he was seeking and stuffed them into the rucksack. He grabbed a bottle of iodine and a bottle of alcohol sitting on a counter and slipped them into the rucksack. He moved to the refrigerator, opened it and examined the bottles of medicine inside. He pulled out several vials holding clear liquid, two clear bags of saline solution and stuffed them into the rucksack. Finally, he picked up a surgical staple gun, slipped it into the rucksack and closed the top. He thought for a moment, then pulled out his wallet and placed fifty Euros on the counter to pay for the supplies he had taken. It wasn't enough to cover the cost of the broken window, but he knew the money in his wallet would have to last for a while since his ATM card and credit cards could easily be traced. Leaving the money made him feel less like a thief.

He moved back into the hallway and saw a German police car with flashing lights and two German police officers out front examining the Humvee. Lowell reversed course and moved to the back of the building. He exited through the back door.

There was a real estate 'for sale' sign in German stuck in the lawn of a dark house. A single light burned in the bathroom window, and the back door was ajar, recently broken.

Lowell sat naked in an empty bathtub. He had rigged a saline drip on to the curtain rod above with the clear tubing leading down into a transfusion needle inserted into his forearm. After only a few minutes of the fluid entering his dehydrated body, he felt better and more awake. He had placed a shaving mirror he had found on the bathroom sink counter on the bathtub faucet. He shaved the hair off his chest around the bullet wound. He stared at his image. What he was about to do was insane, but he couldn't think of any other way.

He used a pair of scissors to cut off the triangular bandage and removed the field dressing covering the bullet wound. He opened the bottle of alcohol, sterilized his hand and the staple gun. He opened another packet of gauze and a large square bandage. He opened a bottle of Vaseline. He opened the package containing a syringe and filled the syringe with the fluid from one of the vials - an antibiotic. He was ready. He injected himself in the chest near the wound and emptied the syringe. He took a deep breath, reached into the bullet wound and pulled out the roll of gauze. He poured iodine into the wound. It bubbled from escaping air. His hands were shaking again. He squeezed the flesh around the hole together, picked up the staple-gun and put three surgical staples in his chest closing the hole. He placed a thick glob of Vaseline over the wound to keep air from entering the wound. He placed the sticky-side of the square bandage over the wound and stuck it to the skin on his freshly shaven chest.

He picked up a large animal syringe with a long needle used to drain fluids from an injury. He placed the syringe and needle over the right side of the top of his chest. He knew he would need to push hard to pierce the sternum. He had watched television shows and movies in which a syringe with a long needle was used to inject adrenaline directly into the heart. He figured this was similar, but he wanted to steer clear of any organs, especially his heart and lungs. He thought a running start would work best. He held the syringe with two hands as far away from his chest as his arms would allow. He plunged the needle into his chest. It disappeared. He was surprised it didn't hurt more. He drew the syringe plunger outward sucking up the excess air around his chest cavity. He immediately felt better and could breathe without a struggle. He removed the needle and placed it on the floor by the tub.

It was done. He was relieved. *Things like that are always worse before you do them than after*, he thought. He slid down into the tub and relaxed. He used the heel of his foot to slip the rubber stopper into the drain and his toes to turn on the hot water. The bathtub filled, the steam rose and Lowell closed his eyes. He didn't think about the hole in his hand which he still needed to treat. He was thinking about Lieutenant Garza. He had to get to her if she was still alive. And if not... revenge the likes of which would make even the devil quiver.

Lowell turned off the water and leaned back in the bathtub. The warm water made him relax and allowed him to think more clearly. He was hungry. He looked over at the pockets on the front and sides of the rucksack and wondered if Miller had stashed a protein bar in one of them. He reached over and drew the pack closer. He rifled through the pockets pulled out the contents. In one of the pockets was a clear plastic ruler identical to the one he had found on Butler. It was non-military issue. Something you would buy at a grocery store or thrift store. Cheap. *Why would Butler and Miller have the same cheap-ass ruler?* he thought. Inside the same pocket were three pages torn from the MGSR map book he had found in the Humvee. There were no markings on the pages. He pulled out the two lists of numbers and letters he had found on the dead MPs. The lists were identical like they had been photocopied from the original. He imagined they were some sort of code, but he had no idea what they meant. The numbers and letters were too long for map coordinates. He placed the ruler on one of the pages thinking it might reveal something. It didn't. *Billy was always good at figuring out this kinda stuff,* he thought. He put the torn map pages, the lists, and the ruler back in the pocket of the rucksack. He could think about them later when he was on the road and he had gotten some sleep. He continued his search for a protein bar and opened the front pouch. He found what he was looking for, ripped open the package and gobbled it down. He also found a prepaid phone still in its plastic packaging in the pocket.

Finishing the last of the protein bar he noticed that the phone's plastic package had been cut open. He wondered why the phone would still be in the packaging. He guessed that someone had charged the phone. He reached into the open slit and pulled the phone out. It was a smartphone and the battery was charged just like he thought. He turned it on and looked through the contacts application. There was only one contact and it was labeled "Six." Six was the radio call sign for the commander of an operation. He pressed the phone number under the contact's name and the phone dialed. "Where the fuck are you are guys? I told you to bury the body not give it a military funeral," said the voice on the other end of the phone. It was a voice Lowell recognized. It was Turner. Lowell's blood ran hot and his mind raced. "Miller, you shit-for-brains, answer me," said Turner.

There was a long silence on the phone. Lowell heard the deep rumble of thunder and the drumbeat of rain on a corrugated roof in the background as he listened. "Miller won't be joining you and neither will Butler," said Lowell.

Another long silence before Turner responded, "I thought it might take more than one bullet to put you down, Lowell. Not really sure why I didn't empty my clip."

"You should have, Master Sergeant. But I promise you... I'm gonna empty mine when we meet again."

"Not if I see you first, Staff Sergeant," said Turner before hanging up.

Lowell was breathing hard and clenching his teeth. He realized he was squeezing the phone so hard he might break it. He set it down and thought. He stared at the water dripping from the bathtub faucet. It gave him an idea. He picked up the phone and opened Google. He typed in, "Extreme weather tracking Germany" and searched the list of websites that appeared. He selected a website and looked down at a list of current extreme weather patterns over Germany. There were only two active thunderstorms. One North, near Berlin and the other West, near Frankfort. Berlin seemed too far, but he decided to check both out, starting with the closest. From the sound of the rain on the corrugated roof, Lowell believed Turner was inside an industrial building or a warehouse of some sort. He doubted that he would be there long. Maybe just waiting for others of his team like Butler and Miller to catch up. A rendezvous point, he thought. He had to go now if he was going to find him.

He rose from the bathtub and removed the saline drip from his arm. He lifted his uniform off the bathroom floor. It was covered in dried blood and shredded where he had ripped it open to examine the bullet wound. He knew he wouldn't get far without someone reporting him to the police.

He moved into the bedroom and examined the closets. They were empty. He moved into the living room and found several moving boxes stacked in the corner. He opened them and found a man's clothes. They were small, but he wasn't picky. He put them on. He grabbed his uniform from the bathroom and stuffed it into the rucksack along with any medical supplies he thought he might need. He picked up Butler's gun and Miller's web belt with the holstered pistol and slipped them into the rucksack. He exited the house with the rucksack over his good shoulder.

TEN

It was night and the rain poured down with the occasional crack of lighting. A rusted flatcar sprayed with German graffiti sat on the railroad tracks next to an abandoned warehouse. The windows had been shattered by mischievous teenagers. The mechanical pulse of a portable generator chugged in the distance. There were floodlights on inside the building.

Inside the warehouse, Thunder sat motionless. The MPs, engineers and technicians were dressed in civilian clothes and busy making preparations with the rain pounding on the roof. "All phones in the drum now," said Turner to the team.

Each member of the team stopped what they were doing and removed their mobile phone's SIM card and battery then broke the phone by smashing it against the rim of an empty oil drum. They dropped the broken phone, the battery, and the SIM card into the drum, then collected a new phone still in its plastic package sitting on a fold-up table. Once the last phone was deposited, Turner removed the SIM and battery from his phone, smashed it and dropped everything into the drum. He pulled the pin on a phosphorous grenade and dropped it on top of the broken phones. The drum lit up like a roman candle incinerating the phones. One by one, the phone batteries exploded from the heat inside the drum. "Let's get back to work," said Turner. The team members moved off to resume work on their assigned tasks.

Several MPs unloaded the truck, carrying the ammunition and equipment stolen from the base into the warehouse, stacking it in two piles.

An engineer wearing a welder's helmet used a cutting torch to burn through the welds on the back of an insulated liquid storage tank mounted on a truck trailer. As he finished with the cutting, several engineers and technicians wearing gloves lifted the stainless steel back off the end of the oval-shaped tank revealing the cavernous and empty interior.

A team of technicians and engineers used a hydraulic pipe cutting machine to slice through 32-inch steel pipes. The shortened segments were stacked on the deck of a railcar next to longer segments of pipe. Another technician glued an enlarged photo of the interior of the pipe to a circular piece of cardboard and glued the cardboard to the end of the shortened length of pipe so if an inspector looked inside the pipe it would appear to be longer than it was and to show all the way to the opposite side; an old magician's trick.

Turner walked over to Specialist Cox and his team of technicians disguising the Sabot and HEAT artillery rounds. Each stack of 30 tank rounds was loaded onto the center of a wooden pallet. A stack of one-liter house paint cans strapped together with steel bands forming an outer façade was lowered over each stack of tank shells. The shells were completely hidden inside the stack of cans. Turner opened one of the paint cans on top of the stack and dipped his finger in the paint. "Outstanding," he said.

The pallets of tank shells with their paint can facades were loaded onto a German delivery truck. Additional pallets holding real paint cans were stacked on top of the façade cans and the cargo doors on the truck were closed. "What's your estimate of how long it will take to reset the delay on the shells?" said Turner.

"It's hard to say," said Cox. "The shells weren't designed for zero delay, so the safety delay ring of each shell has to be altered by hand."

"I didn't ask for a gearhead explanation, Specialist. I asked for your best estimate," said Turner growing impatient.

"Right. Ten to fifteen hours once we reach the rendezvous point," said Cox, unsure.

"Jesus H. Christ, Specialist. How many pee breaks are you planning?"

"It's a delicate operation. Once we set the safety ring to zero delay, the shell basically becomes a live round. Not a lot of room for error."

"Grow some balls and get your ass in gear, soldier," said Turner. "We've got a schedule to keep."

"Yes, Master Sergeant," said Cox. "We'll do our best."

"If I wanted your best, I'd put my boot up your ass which is exactly what's gonna happen if we arrive and that ammunition ain't ready for action," said Turner moving off without waiting for a response.

Inside an office within the abandoned warehouse, a medic pulled back a bloody dressing and examined the forty stitches that held together Garza's wound. She was not happy. "Antibiotics are working. Swelling's gone down," said the medic. "You're gonna be okay, L.T."

"And the scar?" said Garza.

"I made the stitches as tight as I could, but there will be some scarring. I could use petroleum jelly to keep it from forming a scab. That should help with the scarring, but it'll take longer to heal."

"Do it."

"Also, you're gonna want to keep the wound out of the sun as much as possible. No more beach days until it heals," said the medic trying to lighten the mood. It didn't work.

Lowell stood in the convenience store of a gas station watching attendants fuel cars and trucks. He watched the driver of a late model Mercedes leave his car and enter the toilet. The attendant stuck the fueling nozzle in the gas tank and walked off. Lowell walked out to the island, opened the car door and checked the ignition. The keys were in it as he suspected. He removed the nozzle and put it back in its cradle on the pump. He closed the gas hatch and climbed into the car. He started the engine and drove away without anyone noticing. Lowell was no Pollyanna. Still, he didn't like "borrowing" the vehicle. He didn't have much of a choice if he was going to reach Turner before he disappeared again.

It was early in the morning when Billy rode in a taxi to the border crossing between Jordan and Israel. He had Googled an article on the relationship between the two countries and found it interesting. The Jordanians had signed a peace treaty with Israel at the urging of U.S. President Clinton in 1994. Since then, peace and trade had prevailed between the two nations. There was almost a feeling of friendship… almost. The Jordanians were still Arabs and wanted the Israelis to come to an equitable agreement with their Arab brothers, the Palestinians. After twenty-five years of peace between Jordan and Israel that still hadn't happened and the Jordanians were growing weary. Not to mention the pressure the Jordanians were receiving from their surrounding Arab neighbors. But the Jordanians were pragmatic and needed the economic assistance America gave them for being Israel's "friend" in the region. But money would only go so far in placating the Jordanians.

Billy was amazed at how little he knew about the world and international politics. America had played such a central role in the world since the end of World War II, he had forgotten or perhaps never learnt in the first place that other countries also had a large say in what went on, especially in their respective regions. It made him feel ignorant and arrogant. He didn't like it. He was determined to learn what he could about the world while he was traveling.

The taxi crossed a bridge and pulled to a stop in front of a small building with a gate. The words on the sign out in front of the building were written in Hebrew and English. It was the port of entry into Israel. Billy paid the driver. He would take a bus to Jerusalem once he crossed into Israel. He pulled his backpack and messenger satchel from the taxi's trunk and closed the hatch. Everything he owned was in these two bags, except of course his cowboy boots… his most valuable possession apart from his passport. The leather was still damp from his mishap with the rain and the camel in Petra, but they were good boots and he knew they would eventually dry out. He'd need to apply a good amount of boot oil to keep the leather from cracking, but he was sure he could find some in Jerusalem. It was a big city.

Billy got in line inside the building. It wasn't very crowded and most of the people waiting were western tourists that had visited Petra like himself. The line moved quickly. When it was his turn he approached the border guard kiosk and presented his passport. He asked the border guard not to stamp his passport with the Israeli entry stamp, but rather a separate piece of paper that he would carry with his passport to prove that he had legally entered the country. This was a common request. Several Arab countries would deny entry to anyone that had an Israeli entry or exit stamp in their passport. The Israelis were used to this kind of harassment and came up with a simple solution of just stamping a separate piece of paper which the visitor could discard once they left Israel.

The guard stamped a piece of paper, folded it in half and stapled it to one of the empty passport pages. Billy didn't like the staple. Being a nomad, he needed his passport to last more than a normal person and took great care not to damage it. The guard handed back his passport. Billy smiled his thanks and walked out of the building into Israel.

Lowell arrived in the area where the thunderstorm had been reported before sunrise and decided to sleep for one hour to regain some of his strength. He overslept and was awoken by a German farmer tapping on the driver's side window of the Mercedes. At first, Lowell didn't know where he was, but his head quickly cleared. He had unknowingly parked in the farmer's driveway and the farmer wanted him to move his car. Lowell started the car and pulled it forward. The farmer pulled his truck out on to the road and sped off.

Lowell was pissed off that he had overslept. He was trained to operate on very little sleep if necessary, but that was with a healthy body. He was far from healthy and the extra sleep had done him good, even though he wouldn't admit it. He looked in the car's glovebox and found a map of West Germany. He studied the area. There were several towns and a small city nearby. Thunder could be hidden inside a factory or warehouse located in any of them. He decided the small city was probably his best shot because it would most likely have an industrial area. He knew his search was a long shot, but he didn't know how else to find Turner. He slipped the gearshift into drive and drove off in the direction of the city.

Billy stood in the Old City of Jerusalem staring at the wailing wall, known as Kotel in Hebrew and Al-Buraq in Arabic. For Muslims, it was the site where the Islamic Prophet Muhammad tied his steed, al-Buraq, on his night journey to Jerusalem before ascending to paradise, and constituted the western border of al-Haram al-Sharif. To the Jews, Kotel was a retaining wall constructed to expand the second temple built by Herod the Great and later destroyed by the Romans. It was here that the third and final temple would be built signaling the beginning of the age of the Messiah. Throughout history, it had been the most contested religious site in the world.

Billy listened to the cacophony of prayers offered by the Orthodox Jews bowing to the wall. He wondered if God was listening. He wondered about all the humans that had died because of this limestone wall, what it stood for and why it was so important. Clearly, he had some reading to do.

Billy saw a man in the distance walking through the crowd and disappearing. Billy only saw a glimpse of the man and his face wasn't clear, but still, he recognized him. Billy didn't forget faces. He was a natural super matcher which made him unique. There were very few super matchers in the world and they were highly valued by the intelligence communities. The elements of a face were a biometric calculation of angles and distances, broken down, categorized, and placed in a vault in Billy's mind to be recalled at a later time. It was a weird thing, but he couldn't help it. He had learnt to accept it and used it to his advantage.

Billy walked in the direction of where the man had disappeared in the crowd.

Billy walked across a square and sat down at a café next to a man reading a paper in Hebrew. "What do you want?" said Billy without looking at the man.

The man folded the paper revealing his face. It was Culper – the ex-CIA recruiter that once tried to recruit Billy. "What makes you think I want something?" said Culper without looking at Billy.

Billy grunted. "How did you find me?"

"Oh come on, Billy. I wouldn't be much of a handler if I couldn't find one of my subcontractors."

"I keep telling you, I don't work for you," said Billy.

"Of course not. Nobody works for me. Everyone's freelance."

"You put another tracking device in my boot again, didn't you?" said Billy.

Culper shrugged, incredulous, and said, "Why would I do that? You know I trust you."

Billy pulled off his boots and examined them. He found nothing unusual. He thought for a moment, then reached inside each boot and felt something in the right boot up in the toe. He couldn't get his fingers to pry it loose. He pulled his hand out and slammed the heel of the boot against the cobblestone. Nothing came out. He did it again and again until a tracking device wrapped in a sticky-molding clay fell out on to the ground. Billy raised his boot high in the air. "Wait," said Culper. "Those things are expensive."

Billy slammed his boot down on the electronic device, smashing it to pieces. Culper winced. "Why are you here, Culper?" said Billy with growing impatience.

"I've brought news," said Culper. "About your family."

"What about 'em?"

"Your brother is missing."

"Lowell?"

"Yes. He's AWOL… and he's wanted for treason."

"What?" said Billy turning to Culper.

"I thought that might get your attention. Maybe we should go someplace more private, so we can discuss…"

"Stop fucking around and tell me what's going on," said Billy, cutting Culper off.

"Okay. An experimental weapon system was hijacked while on its way to a U.S. Airbase in Germany. The U.S. Army is convinced your brother is part of the hijacking."

"That's insane. Lowell is a little rough around the edges, but he ain't no thief and he sure as hell ain't a traitor. He loves America."

"Okay. That's good to hear," said Culper. "I'm sure they'll straighten it all out once they find him. Sorry to cause you concern, Billy."

Billy studied Culper as he reopened his paper. "You want me to find him? You want me to find Lowell," said Billy.

"To be honest, the thought may have crossed my mind."

"Why can't you just be straight with me?"

"Once a spy always a spy. Honesty is really not in my DNA," said Culper.

"No shit," said Billy. "So what is this weapon system that they think he stole?"

"We call it a hijacking since it was in transit. I can't tell you. It's classified. But if you want to clear your brother, you'd better find it and bring it back."

"Wait. You want me to find something, but won't tell me what it is?"

"Exactly."

"I ain't gonna do it."

"Really?"

"Lowell left my family when we needed him most. He was always a self-serving, narcissistic asshole. I don't owe him anything. He can dig his way out of this mess himself."

"I see. Okay. I'll relay the message to the Army brass. I knew it was a long shot."

"How was I supposed to find him?"

"I don't know. Just do your super matching thing, I suppose."

"This has nothing to do with super matching. I know what Lowell looks like."

"Of course. And you probably know how he thinks too."

"Well yeah. I mean… we did grow up together."

"And there's that. A sibling bond."

"Even if I was to find him, Lowell has never listened to me and he never will. He has a mind of his own and is stubborn as a mule."

"Well, he is your brother…"

"What the hell is that supposed to mean?"

"Nothing. Just making conversation."

"Can I at least talk with the people that think Lowell stole this thing?"

"I suppose I could make some calls."

"Yeah. Do that, will ya?"

"Sure. You might want to go there in person. It makes a better impression. You'd probably get a lot more information out of them."

"Yeah. I should do that… in person."

Billy realized what had just happened and shook his head in disgust. He had been set up to do Culper's bidding… once again.

ELEVEN

It was raining lightly in Belgium, weighing down the trees, filling the streets with leaves.

A dock worker and a shipping manager watched as a large wooden crate was delivered to the building's loading dock. "What the hell is that?" said the dock worker to the shipping manager.

"Some kinda replacement pipe for the water department guys. Better use the freight elevator and take it to the basement."

Two men, De Jong and Meijer, dressed as Water Department repairmen approached the basement's northern wall. Meijer set down a concrete saw with a diamond blade. The wall was marked with a blue chalk outline showing where to cut. Both men put on ear protectors and safety glasses. Meijer started the saw's engine and went to work cutting the concrete wall. It was going to be a big hole.

The dock worker used a palletizer to lower the wooden crate to the basement floor. They spoke in

Dutch. "You want me to open it?" said the dock worker.

"Nah. We got it," said De Jong.

"Watch your toes. It's a heavy bastard," said the dock worker.

"Roger that," said De Jong.

The dock worker removed the palletizer and took the elevator back up to the ground floor. De Jong waited until he was gone before opening the crate. Inside was a 32-inch diameter pipe section with eight Storz couplers for fireman hoses each with its own shutoff value. In the middle of the new pipe section, was a chamber with an access hatch for cleaning the inside of the pipe and a water shutoff valve to one side of the chamber. The chamber had a small glass portal built into the side that allowed those outside the chamber to see the water level inside. De Jong was proud of his design – a custom piece of engineering for a specific purpose.

Esposito wore a business suit as he received last-minute instructions from Turner. "You sure you can trust this guy? It's a lot of money," said Turner.

"He trusted me with his life more than once and I did the same for him. He ain't gonna steer us wrong. I trust him," said Esposito.

"All right. You have the bank wiring instructions?" said Turner.

"Yes, Master Sergeant," said Esposito.

"You need to check and make sure the funds have hit our bank account before you release the delivery."

"Wilco," said Esposito.

"Okay," said Turner as he handed Esposito a new prepaid cell phone still encased in its plastic package. "Good luck, Sergeant."

"Thank you, Master Sergeant," said Esposito as he sat in the driver's seat of an older model Mercedes Benz. "You'll be able to buy yourself a new one of those before long," said Turner with a smile.

"One? Hell. I'm gonna buy an entire fleet of 'em," said Esposito as he drove out of the warehouse.

Fifteen kilometers west of Frankfort, five German police vehicles raced along the autobahn with their lights flashing. The police vehicles changed lanes to form a line across the highway. The line slowed to a stop blocking all the vehicles behind it. The police officers formed a roadblock, setting out traffic cones and directing traffic to a single lane. Passenger vehicles were motioned through the roadblock with only a cursory inspection. Commercial trucks and vans were directed to the side of the road and the contents of each was inspected thoroughly by two police officers. Traffic snarled and long lines formed.

The German police had formed a tight web. Every available officer was assigned to participate in the search for the dangerous weapons the Americans had misplaced. It was a costly operation and the question of who would pay the overtime salaries of the police was a major topic of discussion on the news. Public frustration would grow as the hours ticked on.

The MPs at the U.S. Army base were busy answering phone calls and tracking down leads on Thunder's whereabouts. There wasn't much to go on. Tillman had temporarily turned over the men in his command to Lieutenant Tien. Thunder had been hijacked under his jurisdiction and there would be hell to pay if they didn't find it soon. Even though Tien was younger and he outranked her, he knew she had been trained to investigate this type of crime. She was his best shot at getting his ass out of the frying pan. He also knew that all Tien had to do was pick up the phone and his commanding officer would instruct Tillman to give her whatever she needed to get this mess cleaned up. Tillman decided it was best to offer her the men under his command since she could take them anyway.

Lieutenant Tien sat at her desk examining the photos taken from the crime scene at the meat packing plant. Captain Tillman approached with Billy in tow. Tien closed the folder with the photos and rose. "Lieutenant Tien, this is Billy Gamble. He's Staff Sergeant Gamble's brother," said Tillman. "The CIA sent him over to help us."

"The CIA?" said Tien.

"Yes. I was instructed to give Mr. Gamble our full cooperation. I will leave him in your good hands."

The officers saluted and Tillman retired to his office. "Have a seat, Mr. Gamble," said Tien.

"Billy. Call me Billy."

"You work for the CIA?"

"No. I'm sort of a subcontractor, I guess."

"A subcontractor? Like a mercenary?"

"No. Nothing like that."

"Then what do you do for the CIA?"

"I find people."

"Are you a private investigator?"

"No. More of a rancher. Appaloosas."

"The horses?"

"Yeah. I raise them and train them. I mean, I did… It's been a while."

"So… why does the CIA feel you're qualified to find people?"

"That's a good question. I have no idea. Actually, that's not completely true. I have some idea. They tell me I'm a super matcher."

"A super matcher?"

"I can recognize people's faces by measuring geometric angles and distances. It's something I do unconsciously. There was a man… a serial killer. I found him."

"A serial killer?"

"Yeah. He was in Southeast Asia."

"I wasn't aware that the CIA had an interest in serial killers."

"They don't. As far as I know…"

"You lost me, Billy."

"I wasn't hunting him for the CIA. I was hunting for myself."

"Is that something you do… like a hobby… hunt serial killers?"

"No. He killed someone I knew… Look, what does it matter? I found the guy. The CIA knew I did it and asked me to find someone else… this time for them."

"And you found him?"

"Her. Yes."

"I see. So, you are Sergeant Gamble's brother?"

"Yes."

"Younger or older?"

"Younger. Why does that matter?"

"It doesn't. I was curious. When was the last time you talked with your brother, Billy?"

"At my father's funeral. Twelve years ago."

"Not really close with him, are you?"

"We were, but my father's death changed all that. We had words at the funeral."

"You had a fight?"

"Not a fight. Words."

"I see. So, you haven't talked since then?"

"No."

"What makes you think you can find him?"

"I know him."

"You knew him. People change."

"Not Lowell. He thinks too much of himself to change. I can pretty much guarantee you he's the same self-centered asshole he's always been."

"So, I won't be seeing you as a character witness at his trial?"

"Not likely," said Billy. "You really think it's going to come to that... a trial?"

"The United States Army is not fond of traitors," said Tien.

"Lowell ain't no traitor. I'm sure of that," said Billy.

"If he's such an asshole why do you want to help him?"

"He's family. You don't give up on family."

"No matter what?"

"No matter what."

"So, what can I do for you, Billy?"

"I'd like any information you have and a look at the crime scene."

"No."

"What do you mean... no?"

"I think it's pretty clear."

"You did hear your boss instruct you to cooperate with me?"

"Captain Tillman is not my boss. Did you just try to pull rank on me?"

"No. I didn't try... I did pull rank on you, Lieutenant."

"Billy, I'm in the middle of a murder investigation, not to mention the theft of a very valuable piece of military hardware. I don't have time to play tour guide for an amateur sleuth."

"And my brother's been accused of treason and maybe murder. I don't have time to waste with a stubborn military brat that thinks she's god's gift to the world."

"How'd you know I was a military brat?"

"Your father's photo on your computer's screensaver."

Tien looked at the computer screen facing her and saw the photo with her great-grandfather, McGoon, in his U.S. Air Force uniform. "The screen's not facing you. How did you see it?"

"Your glasses," said Billy.

Tien nodded, impressed. "Are you some kind of cowboy idiot savant?"

"I suppose it depends on who you ask."

"Well, you got it wrong, Cowboy. That's my great-grandfather and I never met the man let alone followed him from base to base."

"Okay. I stand corrected," said Billy. "But you're still stubborn."

"I prefer persistent," said Tien.

"Potato-potato," said Billy. "But I'll concede that persistence is not always a bad trait, especially for a cop."

Tien considered Billy for a long moment. *He could be useful, especially if it comes to getting the Staff Sergeant to surrender without a fight.* "All right, Billy. I'll show you my cards, but only on the condition that you'll do the same if you find out anything new."

"Deal," said Billy.

Billy and Tien walked out of the Military Police office and climbed into a Humvee. Tien drove toward the main gate. "Our armory was robbed just a few minutes after the convoy left the base. We think they were getting ammunition for the weapon system."

"Weapon system?"

"What is your security clearance?"

"I don't know. Culper never told me."

"Who's Culper?"

"He's my handler, I guess."

"For the CIA?"

"Yes."

"Do you even have a security clearance?"

"I don't know. I suppose I must."

"I'm going to need to verify that before we get into any details."

"Probably a smart move."

"We can still talk in general terms. I can tell you everything we told the German police."

"Fine. What weapon system?"

"A new anti-tank drone nicknamed, 'Thunder.' Your brother was the remote operator… and the only one with the access code. The system is useless without the code. Anyway, the guys that robbed the armory stole a bunch of tank rounds used by Thunder, plus a few other things. Enough firepower to start a small, but very deadly war."

"What does anti-tank mean?"

"It was designed to destroy a main battle tank. The Russians have over fifteen thousand still in use. America's got about half that number. Thunder was designed to cut the Russian tank forces down to size if they ever invade NATO. It's a drone so it can stay hidden for days, weeks, even months until it's needed. Thunder uses a sabot-style shell mostly made of depleted uranium. It can penetrate 30 inches of hardened steel, plus any of the new composite armor currently in use."

"Sounds nasty."

"Very."

"So, why steal it?"

"Technology like that could be worth hundreds of millions to the right buyer. I imagine Russians or the Chinese would pay a pretty penny to get their mitts on Thunder. Remember that reconnaissance drone we lost over Iran a few years back?"

"Yeah. It crashed. Something about the Iranians taking over its guidance system."

"Yep. That's the one. Anyway, the Iranians reversed engineered it and in less than three years started cranking out dozens of drones based on our technology. Now they have a whole fleet of them. Some armed too. Sometimes we're our own worst enemy when it comes to leaking weapon technology."

Billy and Tien walked into the meat packing plant. "This is where we found the bodies of two of our MPs. Both had been killed with weapons that had your brother's fingerprints on the handles. There was a 9mm shell casing found on the floor. We also found your brother's blood and the blood from the Lieutenant in charge of the Thunder fields tests. Your brother was severely wounded and lost a lot of blood," said Tien.

Billy walked over and examined the blood on the table and the hole left from the tip of the butcher's steel piercing Lowell's hand. "There were four severed plastic tie straps found on the floor by the chair where we found most of your brother's blood."

"So he could have been tied up?"

"Somebody was. We're testing the straps for DNA. It'll take a few days. There was another tie strap over by the door where we found most of the Lieutenant's blood. We're testing that one too."

"And you don't find that suspicious?"

"Of course I do. But I am not going to draw any conclusions until the test results come back. That's something the Army teaches us in detective school," said Tien with a snarky smile.

"Anything else?"

"We found one of the stolen Humvees with your brother's blood on the steering wheel and seat. It was abandoned in the parking lot of a veterinary clinic. The veterinary clinic had been broken into and medical supplies were stolen. Did your brother know anything about medicine?"

"Only what our parents taught us. Sometimes we had to treat our horses. We couldn't afford to have a vet come out every time one of them got scrapped up. Simple stitching and bandages mostly. First aid stuff. Nothing major."

"Could he have been treating himself?"

"Knowing Lowell... probably. He's one tough cowboy. Didn't particularly like visiting the doctor."

"Good to know."

"What about the other missing soldiers?"

"There are twelve MPs, four engineers and seven technicians all enlisted men, plus the Lieutenant and Master Sergeant Turner."

"A Master Sergeant? That's a pretty high rank, isn't it?"

"Yes. We believe he may have been kidnapped or killed and we just haven't found the body yet."

"Why do you believe that?"

"Master Sergeant Turner had over thirty years of active duty service with multiple decorations and three campaign medals. A Master Sergeant's stripes are not something the Army just hands out. You have to earn them. It's doubtful a Master Sergeant would sacrifice his reputation for money."

"You said the technology could be worth a hundred million or more. That's not chump change."

"True, but we prefer to give him the benefit of the doubt until proven otherwise."

"And my brother?" said Billy.

"Your brother's service record is a little more sketchy. He's one of the oldest Staff Sergeants still wearing a uniform. That too doesn't happen by chance. He was busted in rank a few years back. A bar fight."

"Lowell does love to fight, but that don't make him a traitor."

"We treat everyone as innocent until the evidence says otherwise."

"So have you found any evidence on any of the MPs, engineers or technicians?"

"We have a few things were exploring."

"Mind sharing them?"

"Sure. As soon as we know what they mean."

"In other words... no."

"I prefer not yet. But I'll keep you advised," said Tien. "So, do you have any ideas on where your brother might be?"

"Not yet... but I'll keep you advised."

"What happened to your profound insight?"

"All right. I can tell you this..." said Billy. "You're not going to find Lowell chasing him. He's too smart for that. You've got to get out in front of him. Best way to find Lowell is to find those that stole your gadget."

"That's not real helpful."

"Maybe not... but it's the truth. Can I have a list of the men and women that are missing?"

"Why?"

"I got a hunch."

"I like hunches. Care to share it?"

"Not yet. But I promise I will if it pans out."

"All right. I'll get you the list."

"...and their photos."

"Because you're good at finding people?"

"Yes. If I see one of them, I'll recognize 'em. It's a long shot, but I'm guessing everything's a long shot at this point."

"Good point. I'll get you the list with photos."

Billy rode into town in a Humvee driven by an MP. The driver pulled up to a hotel in the town square. Billy thanked his driver for the lift, grabbed his bags from the back and walked into the hotel.

Billy entered his hotel room and set down his bags. He grabbed an ice water from the minibar and drank half. He pulled out his mobile and dialed. "How's the beer?" said Culper, answering.
"I don't know. I've been too busy,"
"Good to hear. Find anything interesting?"
"Yeah. MP Lieutenants are a pain in the ass."
"Sounds about right. They can be very protective of their turf. You need me to run interference?"
"No. That'll just make it worse. I do need something though."
"Shoot."
"I'm guessing you have a few contacts at the NSA?"
"You'd be guessing right."
"I've got a list of the soldiers that went missing at the same time as Lowell. I'm thinking they're all connected in one way or another. I'd like the NSA to have a look at who they talked with over the phone in the past few months."
"They already did. No arms dealers if that's what you're looking for."
"I don't imagine there would be."
"What do you mean?"
"This thing seems like it was pretty well planned out. I suspect those that planned it would know that we would look at the phone records of the missing soldiers. I don't think they would contact an arms dealer directly and expose their intentions."

"So, what are you looking for?"

"I'm not sure exactly, but I'm guessing one of them contacted an arms dealer indirectly. Through a surrogate. A relative or a longtime friend. Someone they trusted not to betray them."

"I suppose it's possible, but how would we find that out?"

"Work it backward. You must have a list of arms dealers."

"Of course."

"And someone that could pull off a deal of this size should narrow that list considerably."

"It would."

"I'm also guessing the NSA has been listening into their communications for quite a while. Searching for terrorist connections and whatnot."

"Go on."

"So it's like a subway map. We start with the arms dealers that are most likely to pull off a deal like this and we work backward until we find a connection to one of the missing soldiers."

"That's a hell of a lot of work for a hunch, Billy. It's not like I have Carte Blanc with the NSA."

"You want your toy back, don't you?"

Culper thought long and hard before responding, "All right. I'll ask. No guarantee they'll agree though."

"Ask real nice, Culper," said Billy and he hung up.

TWELVE

Inside the abandoned warehouse, Turner watched as the MPs used turnbuckles to tighten the chains that held down a stack of pipes on a flatbed railcar.

Satisfied the pipes were secure, an MP hopped into one of the Humvees and slowly drove the vehicle until its bumper made contact with the railcar's coupler. The Humvee pushed the railcar on the rails in the concrete floor toward a roll-up door at one end of the warehouse. Another MP manually operated the roll-up door that opened to the exterior of the warehouse and the rail spur.

Outside the warehouse, the Humvee's driver carefully pushed the railcar down the tracks of the rail spur. As the railcar approached the main railroad line, the Humvee stopped. The railcar went on for a few more yards and then rolled to a stop. The driver turned the Humvee around and headed back into the warehouse through the roll-up door. The door closed. The railcar sat motionless, waiting…

Billy sat alone on the patio of Thumbach Bierpalast, across the town square from his hotel. He opened the folder Tien had given him and examined each of the photos of the missing soldiers. He unconsciously calculated the angles and distances of each soldier's facial features, so he could easily recognize any of them at a glance. He stopped on Lowell's photo. He hadn't seen Lowell in years and it surprised him how his brother had aged. *I suppose Lowell would think the same of me,* thought Billy. He wondered if enough time had passed that Lowell would think differently about him. After considering the question for a moment, he came to the conclusion that he would not. Lowell was the kind of person that held a grudge for a long time, maybe a lifetime. He considered if he felt the same about Lowell. He did. *Guess we're not that different,* he thought. That thought disturbed him. He didn't like his brother. Sure there were some things about him that Billy admired; Lowell was tough, strong and confident. He acted without hesitation. When he committed to a course of action there was no stopping him; he was like a bull that sees a red flag. But even after all these years, Billy was pretty sure Lowell was still an asshole that only thought of himself. There was no getting around it.

A waitress brought him a beer and set it on the table next to the open folder. "Danke schön," said Billy with a bad accent.

"Bitte. He is your friend?" said the waitress pointing to the photo of Lowell.

"My brother. You know him?"

"Good customer. He likes his beer… and other things."

"Oh. When is the last time you saw him?"

"Two nights ago."

"Was he alone?"

"No. He was with another soldier. A sergeant like him, I think."

"Any of these men?" said Billy rifling through the photos.

"That's him," said the waitress pointing to Turner's photo.

"Did you hear what they were talking about?"

"No. It's a beer hall. People talk. I don't pay attention."

"Right. Thank you for your help."

"You are welcome," she said, walking off.

Billy studied Turner's photo. He placed it next to Lowell's inside the folder and pulled out his mobile.

He dialed the number on Tien's business card clipped to the front of the folder. Tien answered.

"It's Billy. How did Lowell know Turner?"

"That was fast. How'd you figure out that they knew each other?" said Tien.

"Why is every answer a question?" said Billy.

"Habit," she said. "Turner and Lowell served together in Iraq. Turner was the unit commander of Lowell's first assignment. From what we can tell, Turner was Lowell's mentor of sorts. Where are you? It's awfully noisy."

"A beer hall across from my hotel."

"Thumbach Bierpalast?"

"Yeah. How'd you know?"

"It's the beer garden where most of the off-duty personnel from the base hang out," said Tien, then stopping to think… "They were there, weren't they?"

"Yeah. A couple nights ago… before the robbery."

"Hijacking," said Tien correcting him.

"Okay. Hijacking. Probably just two old friends catching up."

"Or going over last minute details."

"He didn't do it, Lieutenant Tien. I know my brother."

"Yeah. Well, I'm sure Jesse James' mom liked him too. Call me when you find something important." Tien hung up.

Tien pissed Billy off. She was rude and aggressive when she didn't need to be. He wondered if it was because she was a woman or maybe because she was Asian. She was nothing like the Asian women he had known. She was nothing like Noi. But why should she be? *Maybe I'm the asshole,* he thought.

Outside the abandoned warehouse, the railcar loaded with steel water pipes sat. Two MPs hidden nearby in the bushes watched over the railcar with night-vision binoculars.

A freight locomotive pulling several railcars stopped near the rail junction. The conductor jumped off and opened the switch to the rail spur. The locomotive backed up until the rear coupler on its last railcar hit the waiting railcar's coupler. The conductor connected the pneumatic and electrical lines between the two. He stepped out from between the railcars and signaled the locomotive operator that the new railcar was connected. The locomotive pulled the railcars on to the main track. The conductor switched back the rail spur track and hopped back on the locomotive. The train drove down the main track until it disappeared around a corner. The MPs moved off into the darkness, unseen.

Lowell sat in a small town diner eating a steak. His blood needed the iron. It hurt to chew. His wounds were healing, but his body was reminding him to take it easy. He wasn't listening and pushed himself as long and as hard as he could, until fatigue overwhelmed him and he was on the verge of collapse. It didn't take much. Food helped. Coffee helped more. He drank a lot of coffee. What he really wanted was a bottle of Jack Daniels, but he knew that wouldn't help his body or his mind. He needed to stay focused. He wondered about Garza. Was she still alive? He supposed that if Turner was going to kill her, he would have done it at the meat packing plant where he thought he had killed him. At least that was the hope. He wondered how Turner would use her and what dangers she could face. He like Garza a lot more than he thought. Did he love her? *Fuck no,* he thought. *Love is for pussies.* But the thought of settling down with one woman didn't seem so farfetched when he thought about Garza. *She'd probably want babies and her boobs would sag from nursing them,* he thought. She'd get fat and ignore him. Or worse, try to control him. He could see them fighting over the television remote and her yelling at him when he ate the cherry tomatoes out of her salad plate without asking. It all felt like a divorce waiting to happen. Still… she had nice teeth.

The map of the area was laid out on the table in front of him. A few drops of syrup from the side of pancakes he had ordered had dripped on the map. He wiped the sticky drops off with his fingers and licked them. He had drawn "Xs" through the quadrants he had searched. There were still a lot of areas he hadn't gotten to yet. It was a time-consuming process going building to building, hoping to see something that would alert him to Thunder's whereabouts. He had little faith that Turner and his team were still there, but he thought he could at least look for clues as to their whereabouts. Maybe they'd abandoned Garza and he'd find her tied up and gagged. It would be good to see her again. *It's a long shot, but it could happen,* he thought. It was the only thing he could think to do and he knew he had to do something. He folded up the map, finished his meal and paid the bill.

He carried Miller's rucksack into the toilet and locked the door. He had been sleeping in the Mercedes. It wasn't too bad with the seat reclined all the way back. He smelled pretty rank, but he didn't care. Still, he didn't want to draw any more attention than absolutely necessary. He used wet paper towels to give himself a quick whore's bath. He pulled off his shirt and the bandages on his chest and hand. The bruise around the bullet hole was dark purple and brown like the time he had been kicked in the chest by a bull after falling off the back of the beast. The antibiotics he had stolen from the clinic and injected around the wounds had done their job and there was little sign of infection. The wounds had scabbed over. He pulled out a bottle of hydrogen peroxide he had bought and poured it over the wounds on his chest and hand. It bubbled, killing the bacteria and dissolved the dead skin. He rewrapped his wounds with fresh bandages and left the toilet.

As he walked out of the toilet back into the diner, Lowell froze. Through the windows, Lowell saw a German police car pull up to the diner and park next to the Mercedes. Two police officers stepped out. One glanced over at the Mercedes and took a peek inside. Lowell remembered he had left Miller's web belt with his holstered pistol sitting on the floor in front of the passenger seat. The officer looking in the Mercedes said something to the other officer and laughed. It seemed like small talk about the late model car, but Lowell couldn't be sure. The officers walked through the front door into the diner. The diner was crowded and the officers stood near the doorway waiting for a seat.

Lowell lowered his head and moved over to a rack of candy near the cash register like he was shopping. With his head lowered, he looked down at his chest. There was a circle of blood growing on his shirt. His thought was that the blood had already seeped through the new chest bandage and was now soaking through his shirt. He casually turned away from the doorway and started to zip up his jacket to cover the growing blood spot.

One of the officers walked toward him. Lowell stopped zipping up the jacket. He had Butler's pistol tucked in the back of his pants, covered by his jacket. He thought about pulling it out. He knew he wouldn't use it against the officers. They were just doing their job and he couldn't justify hurting them, but maybe he could bluff his way out by brandishing the gun. He decided against it. Too much risk of getting into a firefight around civilians. He would let the officers arrest him and accept the consequences. The officer moved past him into the toilet. Lowell finished zipping up his jacket, walked past the other officer and out of the diner. He climbed into Mercedes, started the engine and drove off careful to obey the traffic laws.

In the park near his hotel, Billy finished his lunch. He opened his sandwich, pulled out the ham, lettuce, and tomato and popped them into his mouth. He used the remaining sandwich bread to feed a group of ducks patiently gathering around. His phone rang. He looked at the Caller ID – It was Culper. "Find anything?" said Billy answering the call.

"You're in luck. Esposito, the sergeant in charge of the MP platoon, has been talking with an Edward Laurent. They served together in Afghanistan. After two tours in Afghanistan, Sergeant Laurent retired and joined Blackwater in Iraq. He was assigned to protect an oil refinery in the Northern territories.

Apparently, babysitting a bunch of pipes filled with oil wasn't the same as fighting the Taliban in the mountains of Tora Bora. He lasted one year, quit and went the mercenary route. Hired gun to the highest bidder. Esposito and Laurent have kept in contact over the years. Six months ago, Laurent started making inquiries about selling excess U.S. Army weapons and ammunition to the black market. That's when he shows up on our radar. He made contact with an arms dealer named Jarek Svoboda working out of Pilsen, Czech Republic. Svoboda mostly sells to West African nations with a few deals in Ukraine and with the Kurds in Northern Iraq. He's a pretty big player and known for handling heavy equipment."

"Great. That's your guy. Set up a trap and arrest him."

"I wish it were that easy. Turns out CIA wants nothing to do with him."

"What? Why?"

"Hard to say, but if I had to guess... I'd say he knows too much and they're afraid he might say something indiscreet."

"You mean like they're doing business with the guy?"

"Probably. Yeah. They don't tell me everything these days since I've gone freelance and all."

"So, what are you going to do?"

"Nothing."

"Nothing? I thought the whole point was for you to find Thunder and return it, so Lowell is off the hook," said Billy.

"Me, no. You, yes. And I'd appreciate it if you kept my name out of it from this point on."

"What the hell is that supposed to mean?"

"The deal is the same as I explained it. You find Thunder, return it and your brother is cleared of any charges assuming he's not in on the hijacking. You get to go on your merry way knowing that you served your country and helped your family."

"How am I supposed to stop a bunch of rogue soldiers armed to the teeth?"

"Personally, I'd buddy up with the Army. They seem pretty determined to get Thunder back and bring the bad guys to justice."

"They don't trust me and they sure as hell aren't gonna listen to my suggestions."

"It may take some convincing..."

"Convincing? Are you insane?"

"Insanity is a very subjective term."

Billy took a moment to regain his composure. "Do you have a photo and an address for this Jared Svoboda?"

"It's Jarek, not Jared and yes I do. I'll text them to you. Keep me posted, will ya?"

"Fuck you, Culper," said Billy, and he hung up.

Culper had a bad habit of getting Billy into a situation, then pulling out the rug from underneath him. *I don't need this shit,* Billy thought. *This is Lowell's mess, not mine.* That was the truth of it and Billy thought about just chucking the whole thing back in Culper's lap. But Lowell was family and Billy had been taught that family was important even if they were a pain in the ass. His father would have wanted him to help Lowell no matter the cost, and Billy loved his father. So, there it was... Billy had no choice but to continue his search for Lowell and Thunder on his own.

A freight train approached the Czech border crossing and pulled to a stop. Accompanied by the train's conductor, two Czech border guards armed with submachine guns walked along the freight cars inspecting the exterior of each car and searching the undercarriage for stowaways. The guards randomly selected a few boxcars and the conductor unlocked and opened the doors allowing them to inspect the interiors.

When the border guards came to the flatcar carrying the steel pipes, one of the guards pulled out his flashlight and inspected each of the pipes for stowaways. When he shined his flashlight inside the shortened pipes with the enlarged photo covering the back end, it appeared the pipes went all the way through and he gave them no special attention.

After inspecting the last car, the border guards gave the conductor permission to cross into the Czech Republic and the train pulled through the border crossing without incident.

When Billy walked into the MP office he knew that without Culper's help he was up shit creek without a paddle. He had one piece of information that he needed to leverage to the hilt if he was to have any hope of finding and helping Lowell. As uncomfortable as it felt, Billy had concluded that he needed help.

Tien hardly looked up from her desk as Billy approached. To her, he was dead weight. "How can I help you, Mr. Gamble?" said Tien keeping her eyes on her paperwork, refusing to give him the respect of looking him in the eye.

"I asked you to call me Billy," said Billy.

"Sorry. Force of habit. What do you want… Billy? I'm kinda busy."

"I told you I would keep you advised if I found something."

"And?"

"Sergeant Esposito has been using a surrogate to communicate with a Czech arms dealer."

Tien stopped what she was doing, looked up at Billy and said, "Okay. You've got my attention. How do you know this?"

"I can't say, but I think you can guess."

"CIA? NSA?"

"Like I said… I can't say."

"So, that was your hunch?"

"That and a few other things I'm still working on."

"Okay, good work. We'll put a surveillance team on the arms dealer and wait for Esposito to show up."

"No, you won't."

"What do you mean?"

"I don't want a bunch of undercover MPs sneaking around and maybe tipping this guy off. This is my lead. I'll check it out on my own… and keep you advised."

"You said yourself, you're not a professional."

"I'm not. And at times that works in my favor. This is one of those times. I'll give you a call when I confirm Esposito's whereabouts," said Billy starting to walk away.

"Wait… maybe we can work something out."

"You've got nothing I want or need, Lieutenant. This was a courtesy call. I am a man of my word."

"You can have a look at our files."

Billy stopped and considered. "All of them?"

"I can't show you any of the top secret stuff, but everything else will be made available to you. Plus, you're gonna need some firepower if you actually find Thunder. They're not just going to give it up. And believe me, it's a force to be reckoned with."

"Interesting… I still don't want a bunch of MPs tipping him off."

"I understand. Just me, until we confirm Thunder's whereabouts and bring in reinforcements."

"Can you take orders from a man?"

"Don't push it, Billy."

"Yeah. I thought that might be going too far," said Billy with a smile. "All right. You got a deal."

They shook hands wearily. "Pack light. The bullet train for Pilsen leaves in two hours."

"Copy that."

Billy moved off and said, "Meet me at the train station at O-Sixteen-hundred and don't forget those files you promised."

Billy stood on the train platform looking for signs of Tien. The bullet train had already pulled up and he was concerned that it might leave without them. Tien, dressed in civilian clothes, appeared from a stairwell. She had her rucksack on her back and was carrying two U.S. Army shipping cases. "Sorry, I'm late," she said. "I had to make a stop."

"I already have the tickets, so let's go. I thought I asked you to pack light."

"I did. But if we stumble upon Thunder, you're gonna be glad we have this."

"What is it?"

"A javelin."

Billy didn't have time to play guessing games. He helped her lift the shipping cases onto the waiting train and they boarded just before the doors closed for departure.

The bullet train glided through the countryside at 180 kilometers per hour. Inside, Tien slept. Billy went through the service records of the missing soldiers that she had given him. He examined their history, commendations and progress reports; anything that would give him insight into who they might be and where they might be.

Billy looked over at Tien sleeping. He thought for a moment, then got up and moved through the train to the dining car. He ordered a cappuccino, pulled out his mobile and dialed. Culper answered. "It's Billy. You need to rethink your involvement."

"Why?"

"I think there is something bigger going on here than just a weapon heist."

"Like what?"

"I'm not sure yet, but I don't know who I can trust."

There was a long pause on the phone line. "What do you need?" said Culper.

THIRTEEN

Billy and Tien sat by the window of a Pilsen hotel room watching the street below. The sheers were drawn to prevent anyone outside from seeing them as they watched. When they saw something of interest they would spread the opening between the sheer panels to get a better look.

A limousine pulled up in front of an office building across the street from the hotel. The driver got out and opened the back door for his passenger, a man dressed in a business suit.

"That's him," said Billy. "That's Jarek Svoboda."

"Nice suit," said Tien.

"War pays good," said Billy.

"No. It really doesn't," said Tien. "Just ask my mortgage broker."

Svoboda disappeared into the office building. "It could take a while before Esposito shows. If he shows at all," said Tien.

"I don't know about that," said Billy.

"How's that?"

"I would think they would want to unload their merchandise as fast as possible."

"Maybe. But Thunder's not just any merchandise. It's very valuable, but only to a handful of buyers."

"Yeah, but these guys have probably been planning all of this for quite a while," said Billy.

"Probably, but why do you think that?"

"When you looked at all the service records of the MPs, engineers, and technicians that have gone missing, did you notice anything peculiar?"

"You mean that they all transferred into the Military Police from other branches of the Army?"

"Yeah."

She nodded. "We noticed."

"It took time to get them all transferred to the same unit. All serving at the same base at the same time and just in time for Thunder's field test."

"Your point?"

"They had time to set up a deal. It's possible it was even a special order. My guess is that they're gonna delivery as fast as possible, collect their money and get the hell out of Dodge."

"Nice bit of conjecture."

"There's one more thing…"

"What's that?"

"So far the highest ranking soldier that is missing is the lieutenant, right?"

"Technically, yes. Although Master Sergeant Turner would be considered more powerful and influential than Lieutenant Garza, technically she still outranks him."

"Okay. Do either Master Sergeant Turner or Lieutenant Garza have the authority to transfer soldiers from various units?"

"No… they don't."

"Then there has to be another officer involved. Someone with the authority to transfer those soldiers. Who might that be?"

"I don't know offhand, but I'll check into it."

"I doubt whoever it was signed the transfers themselves. Once you find the connections, you might want to look upstream a bit."

"We're talking a pretty high rank, you know."

"Yep. The thought had occurred to me. Discretion would be the better part of valor in this case."

"Ya, think? This is the kinda thing that can kill a military career if I accuse the wrong officer."

"Let's not be wrong then," said Billy. "I'll take the first watch and you can catch some shuteye."

"Yeah, like I could sleep right now. I'll take the first watch."

"Suit yourself."

Billy pulled off his boots and lay down on the bed. He was asleep in less than a minute. Tien looked over at him as he began to snore. "Cowboys," she said to herself shaking her head. She wasn't sure how she felt about Billy. She liked that he was straightforward and said what he thought. She could tell he was smart. She found him strangely attractive. When the thought hit her, she immediately drove it out of her mind. She had no time for any kind of romantic encounter, especially when it was someone she was unsure about. After all, one of her prime suspects was Billy's brother. She made a new rule – No sex with Billy. She liked rules and made them up often. They kept her grounded and focused on the job at hand. She had lived her life by the unspoken rules of her culture and family. Obedience was a form of respect.

On the street below, a heating and cooling company van drove past the office building and pulled into an alley beside the building.

The van pulled into the building's loading dock and parked. Two repairmen, Mason and Hughes, wearing company-issued coveralls got out and opened up the back doors to the van. They took out their tool belts and a heavy shipping case. A building manager walked out a doorway. They spoke in Czech. "Are you guys with the air conditioning company?" said the building manager.

"That's right," said Mason.

"What's the big rush? It seems to be working fine," said the building manager.

"Preventative maintenance. Factory recalled a faulty condenser unit. We just want to swap it out now and head off any future breakdowns," said Mason.

"Great. I don't need problems," said the manager. "Do you need me to go up with you?"

"No. We got it. Just point us in the right direction."

"Freight elevator goes to the top floor. Just take the stairwell to the roof. Door's unlocked. Call me if you need anything," said the building manager handing Mason his business card.

"Got it," said Mason as he slid the card into his pocket.

The two repairmen carried the shipping case out of the stairwell on to the roof and over to the air conditioning unit. They opened the case and removed a portable IMSI CATCHER - a cellular surveillance repeater that hijacked nearby mobile signals and relayed the signals without the mobile phone owner knowing their communications were being monitored.

They set up the IMSI Catcher unit on a tripod at the edge of the rooftop behind the air-conditioning unit so it wasn't easily visible. Then they turned the unit on and monitored its progress as it hijacked hundreds of mobile phone signals. Mason pulled out his mobile phone and dialed. Hughes monitored the IMSI Catcher on a laptop computer. He typed in a keyword phrase – Test One - into the computer and nodded to Mason. "Test One," said Mason into his phone.

Hughes watched the signal as it showed up on his computer screen and displayed the caller's and the receiver's locations. "We're good," said Hughes.

Mason hung up his mobile. They closed the empty shipping case and carried it away.

Mason drove the van around the corner from the office building and parked on a side street. He moved to the back of the van where Hughes was inputting keywords into the laptop computer. "How's it going?" said Mason.

"Almost done," said Hughes as he keyed in the final words and phrases from a long list – Laurent, Esposito, Turner, Master Sergeant, Staff Sergeant, Lieutenant, Gamble, and Thunder.

It was night and Tien was asleep on the bed when Billy, watching through the hotel window, spotted Esposito and Edward Laurent walking into the office building. "Lieutenant?" said Billy.

Tien woke up and said, "What's up?"

"Esposito and Laurent just walked into the building."

"That didn't take long. You were right."

"We should get moving downstairs."

"Yeah. Why don't you pull the rental car into the alley? I'm gonna splash some water on my face."

"Five minutes?"

"Copy that."

Billy left the room. Tien dialed a number on her mobile phone and waited until a man answered, "Hello?"

"It's Tien. We are go."

Inside the office building, Esposito dialed a number on the new prepaid mobile phone that Turner had given him. Turner answered. "We just arrived at Svoboda's office. I'm guessing it will take another thirty to forty minutes before he inspects the shipment and wires the money," said Esposito into the mobile.

"Good, Sergeant," said Turner. "Keep me posted."

"Roger that, Master Sergeant," said Esposito and hung up.

On the rooftop, the IMSI Catcher processed the mobile's signal.

In the van, Hughes watched the computer monitor as an alert message flashed on the screen – Keyword 'Master Sergeant' Activated. "We gotta a hit," said Hughes.

"Do you have a location?" said Mason, anxious.

"Processing now," said Hughes. "Bingo. Looks like the receiver is in a small town just outside of Frankfurt."

Mason dialed his mobile. Culper answered. "We got 'em," said Mason.

"Excellent," said Culper.

Billy and Tien sat in a rental car watching the building as Svoboda's limousine pulled up and parked on the street. Esposito, Laurent, Svoboda carrying a laptop bag, and three bodyguards armed with submachine guns, exited the building. Laurent rode with Svoboda and the bodyguards in his limousine while Esposito followed in his Mercedes.

Billy and Tien followed at a distance, careful not to give themselves away.

Unseen by all of them, a fourth vehicle - a windowless sprinter van - followed even farther behind the group.

Svoboda's limousine and Esposito's Mercedes drove through an industrial area and over a set of railroad tracks.

With few vehicles on the roads in the industrial area, Billy and Tien were forced to put more distance between themselves and their prey to avoid being detected.

Svoboda's limousine and Esposito's Mercedes slowed and parked in front of a warehouse. An automatic roll-up door opened and they entered the building on foot. One of Svoboda's bodyguards walked back through the open doorway and stood guard outside the building as the roll-up door closed.

Billy and Tien parked their car and approached on foot. Tien glanced back down the road and caught a glimpse of the windowless Sprinter van pulling over and turning off its lights. She made no mention of it.

Billy and Tien moved off into the foliage alongside the road to hide their approach to the warehouse.

They moved to the side of the warehouse out of sight of the bodyguard in front. Billy found a door on the side of the building. It was locked. "You any good at picking locks?" said Billy.

"What's wrong? Didn't they teach that kinda stuff in spy school?" said Tien pulling out a lock pick kit and going to work on the door's lock.

"Like I said… I'm not a spy," said Billy.

Tien picked the lock and the door swung open.

Tien and Billy entered the warehouse. They were in a group of offices with windows. They kept low and out of sight. Through several layers of office windows, they could see the main part of the warehouse.

A roll-up door on the back wall of the warehouse opened. A Unimog railcar shunter pushed the flatcar with the water pipes into the warehouse on a set of rails mounted in the concrete floor. The flatcar rolled to a stop. The Unimog disengaged the flatcar and disappeared back out the way it came through the roll-up door. The door closed.

A forklift drove to the side of the railcar and placed its fork perpendicular to the top layer of pipes. Two workers detached the turnbuckles and removed the chains that held the stack of pipes in place. They used a small overhead crane attached to a ceiling support beam to lift the pipes from the top of the stack and placed them on the forklift revealing the contents of the hidden chamber inside the stack of pipes.

From their vantage point, Tien and Billy could not see the contents of the hidden chamber. "We need to find a better angle," said Billy as he moved off.

Billy found a stairway and motioned to Tien to get her attention without making any noise. They climbed up to the second story.

Svoboda climbed up onto the flatcar and carefully climbed up the side of the pipes and into the hidden chamber, to inspect what he was purchasing.

Even on the second story, Billy and Tien could not see inside the hidden chamber within the stack of pipes. As Billy watched the activities inside of the warehouse, Tien discretely sent a text on her mobile phone. It read: Take up breaching positions and hold for my signal.

Back on the road, the doors of the Sprinter van opened. Eleven heavily armed Czech URNA agents along with a U.S. Army advisor climbed out of the van and moved quietly toward the warehouse using the foliage on the side of the road as cover.

Svoboda climbed out of the hidden chamber and back down to the concrete floor of the warehouse. He nodded to Esposito and Laurent that he was satisfied with the delivery. He opened his laptop to finish the wiring of funds. Esposito dialed his mobile phone.

Outside the warehouse, a URNA sniper shot the bodyguard keeping watch in the front of the building with his silenced rifle. The armor-piercing bullet went through the bodyguard's Kevlar vest and straight through his heart. The bodyguard collapsed, dead, without so much as a whimper. The URNA unit divided into fire teams and surrounded the building on all sides.

Turner watched the progress of preparations in the abandoned warehouse when his phone rang. He answered it and listened. "The transaction is complete, Master Sergeant. You should be able to verify the funds," said Esposito over the phone.

"Hold the line, Sergeant," said Turner and put the call on hold.

Turner used his smartphone to access a bank account. The balance on the screen changed from three hundred Euros to Nine hundred and fifty thousand Euros. He smiled and took the smartphone off hold. "Funds are verified. Outstanding work, Sergeant Esposito. Now get your ass in gear and meet us at the rendezvous point," said Turner.

"Copy that, Master Sergeant," said Esposito, and he hung up.

Tien and Billy watched from their perch on the second floor of the abandoned warehouse. "I think they just wired the funds," said Billy.

"I agree," said Tien entering the text – Execute – into her phone and pressing send.

Inside the warehouse, Esposito pulled a remote detonator from his pocket and flipped the switch from 'Armed' to 'Safe.' "What's that?" said Svoboda.

"My insurance policy. Remote detonator for twenty-pounds of C-4 in the bottom of one of the ammunition cases," said Esposito. "You can keep it. No extra charge."

"What the fuck?" said Svoboda.

"Relax. I was just keeping everyone honest," said Esposito. "You guys got what you wanted and my guys got what we wanted. Everyone's happy."

"What about my commission?" said Laurent.

"Like I told you, you'll get it in a couple of days," said Esposito.

"Fuck that," said Laurent and pulled out a pistol from his jacket. "Nobody leaves until I get my cut."

"That wasn't the deal, Laurent," said Esposito. "You get paid when I get paid."

"This is the new deal. I get paid now," said Laurent.

"Fine. You've got a bank account that I can transfer it to?" said Esposito and redialed Turner's smartphone.

On the second floor, Billy's phone vibrated. It was a text message from Culper, reading – Turner accessed bank account using his smartphone. Nine hundred and fifty thousand Euros just deposited by wire transfer. "It's not enough," said Billy.

"What's not enough?" said Tien.

"Turner just received nine hundred and fifty thousand Euros by wire transfer. That's not nearly enough."

"Maybe it's a down payment."

"Maybe, but then that's not Thunder down there."

"Oh shit," said Tien pulling out her mobile phone and dialing.

"What are you doing?"
"I've got to stop them."
"Stop who?" said Billy.

It was too late. Breach charges exploded on the outer doors of the warehouse and the URNA fire teams rushed in from all sides with their weapons leveled. Flashbang grenades rolled across the concrete floor and exploded with bright flashes of light and deafening cracks.

Esposito and Laurent dove for cover as they had been trained to do.

Svoboda's bodyguards stood their ground and fired back at the advancing URNA officers. Svoboda threw up his hands in surrender.

The URNA opened fire, cutting the bodyguards down and Svoboda with them.

Laurent fired at the URNA from his covered position behind the wheel of the flatcar. Bullets ricocheted off the steel wheels and the edge of the flatcar.

Esposito was hidden behind the forklift ten yards away and could see that Laurent was pinned down. He looked for a way out and spotted an open door. "Sorry, Laurent," he yelled as he ran for the door, flipped the switch to "Armed" on the remote detonator and squeezed the trigger.

Closest to the C-4, Laurent was killed in an instant by the explosion. Steel water pipes flew through the air, knocking down URNA agents like human bowling pins.

The windows in the offices shattered showering Billy and Tien with glass shards as they ducked behind a desk.

Esposito was knocked off his feet from the concussive wave and slid across the concrete floor. He stopped sliding just a few feet from the open door, unconscious.

Billy moved to where Tien lay face down on the floor covered in shards of window glass. "Are you all right?" said Billy.

"I think so," said Tien, unsure.

Billy and Tien got up from behind the desk and looked out into the warehouse. Anything that was flammable was burning. The flatcar was demolished and empty. Pieces of Laurent were everywhere. URNA agents were laying on the floor, some motionless, others struggling to their feet. On the opposite side of the warehouse, Billy could see Esposito struggling to his feet and picking up his pistol, blood seeping from his ears and eyes. He stumbled through the open doorway and escaped the mayhem.

"Stay here," said Billy.

"Where in the hell are you going?" said Tien.

"Esposito," said Billy as he vanished down the stairway.

Outside, Esposito came around the corner to the front of the warehouse just as Billy came around the opposite corner. It hadn't dawned on Billy that he was unarmed and that Esposito was armed. He just knew he had to stop Esposito or he would lose any chance of finding Lowell.

Esposito was still dazed from the explosion and wobbled toward his Mercedes. As he fumbled for his car keys with one hand he fired two shots at Billy with the pistol in his other hand.

Billy hit the ground as the shots zinged over his head. He saw two rocks in front of his face. He grabbed them and scrambled to his feet. Billy had played baseball in high school and had a pretty good arm back in the day. He threw the first rock overhand like a pitch. It missed Esposito completely and slammed into the windshield of the Mercedes shattering the safety glass in front of the driver's seat.

Billy ducked behind the edge of the building as Esposito fired another round in his direction. He readied the second rock in his right hand. He swung around just as Esposito dropped into the driver's seat and pulled the door closed. The rock smashed into the driver's side and shattered the door's window into a spider web of glass pieces. Esposito ignored Billy, started the engine and slammed the gearshift into reverse. The Mercedes sped backward toward the road.

Billy was out of rocks, so he ran after the car.

Esposito really wanted to stop the car, get out and shoot Billy but knew his escape was more important. The Mercedes skidded sideways into the street as Esposito cranked the wheel. Esposito slammed the gearshift into drive and floored the gas pedal just as Billy reached the street. The Mercedes jerked forward and gained speed as it headed toward the road. Billy ran after it like a dog chasing a bicycle. As the Mercedes gained speed, Billy jumped onto the trunk and grabbed onto the edge of the hatch.

Esposito had trouble seeing the road through the shattered windshield and side window. He glanced at the rearview mirror and saw Billy on the trunk. "God damn it," said Esposito as he fired three rounds at the back window, shattering it.

Esposito turned around in the seat, leveled his gun and took aim at Billy's head. Billy saw something out of the corner of his eye that made him let go of the trunk hood and it wasn't Esposito. He tumbled across the gravel road.

Esposito took another shot at Billy that missed and turned back around, satisfied he was rid of the threat. He did not see the freight train speeding towards the street crossing or the red blinking lights through the Mercedes' shattered windshield and side window.

The locomotive t-boned the Mercedes on the driver's side crushing Esposito. The vehicle was launched from the tracks and tumbled into a chain link fence.

Billy ran over to the wrecked Mercedes in hopes that Esposito was still alive. He wasn't. Billy cursed.

FOURTEEN

An MP dressed as a civilian in uniform drove a truck pulling two spotless stainless steel tanker trailers from the abandoned warehouse. On the side of each of the tankers was an advertisement with the enlarged photo of a smiling mom watching her son drink a glass of milk. Turner, Garza, and the rest of the MPs, engineers and technicians, all dressed as tourists, rode in a passenger sprinter van with a tour company's decal on each side. The truck pulling the trailers crossed the railroad tracks and pulled on to the main road. The van followed at a distance.

Sitting in a passenger seat in the van, Turner pulled out his smartphone and removed the SIM chip and the battery. He lowered the window and threw the phone into the woods alongside the road. He waited twenty seconds then threw the SIM chip and the battery out the window and into the trees. He raised the window back up and sat back to catch some shuteye.

Billy and Tien sat on the bumper of a paramedic truck as a German paramedic treated the scrapes and cuts caused by the explosion. "I don't get it," said Billy.

"Get what?" said Tien

"Why risk selling stolen arms to an arms dealer?"

"Nine hundred and fifty thousand Euros seems like a good reason."

"Normally, yes. But you said Thunder could be worth over a hundred million."

"Or more," said Tien.

"So, it's like dollar waiting on a dime. Why take the risk for an amount so small? Why not just cash out on the big payday and call it a day?"

"Maybe they needed a quick cash injection to finance their operation," said Tien.

"Or maybe they needed to buy something," said Billy.

"Like what?"

"I don't know. But they must have had a reason to take a risk like that." Billy got up.

"Where are you going?"

"To find my brother."

"Hang on. I'll go with you."

"No."

"What do you mean, no?"

"I can't trust you."

"You can't trust me?" said Tien, surprised.

"We had an agreement and you broke it."

"What are you talking about?"

"The URNA agents that raided the warehouse were tipped off."

"And you think I did it?" said Tien, incredulous.

Billy didn't respond. Tien squirmed, then said, "Okay. I may have… No… I did tip them off. And I know I said I wouldn't bring in any of my MPs, but technically I didn't."

"Technically?"

"Look… I couldn't risk losing Thunder again."

"How'd that work out for you?"

"My job is to get that weapon system back before it's used to wreak havoc. I'm sorry if I stepped on your toes."

"You burned the best chance we had at finding Thunder… and my brother."

"With hindsight… I admit I may have made a mistake and acted prematurely. But remember, you're gonna need me and my soldiers if you find Thunder and Turner."

"Good luck, Lieutenant," said Billy walking off.

"Billy, come on… we work good together."

"Did, Lieutenant. We did," said Billy not looking back as he exited the building.

Once outside the warehouse, Billy pulled out his phone and made a call. Culper answered. "Do you have the location of Turner's last phone call?"

"Yep. I'll text it to you," said Culper.

"Thanks," said Billy and hung up.

Billy waved down a passing truck and hitched a ride.

The truck dropped Billy off at the hotel, where he gathered his things from the room. Then he checked the train schedules on his phone and took a taxi to the station.

He bought a ticket on the next high-speed train to Frankfort. He considered taking a plane. It was faster than the train, but it would require a trip to and from the airports, both of which were located outside the cities. That idea ended up a washout when he included the additional travel time in a taxi. He chose the train. He thought better on trains. There was plenty of leg-room so he could stretch out. He had only had a few short naps in the last couple of day and needed some real sleep. He doubted he would get much sleep once he got to Frankfort.

He arrived on the platform a couple of minutes before the train was due to depart. He boarded, found his seat, stowed his backpack and messenger satchel on the overhead rack, sat down by the window and was asleep before the train pulled out of the station. Billy could sleep anywhere when he put his mind to it.

The milk tanker truck sat in a long line waiting its turn at a German police roadblock. A fire team from a nearby German Army base was stationed in their armed vehicle to the side of the roadblock. One of the soldiers had a shoulder-launched anti-tank missile at the ready, just in case. Passenger cars were waved through quickly by the police, while any vehicle big enough to hide Thunder was waved to the side of the autobahn and thoroughly searched. A police officer waved the tanker forward.

Several vehicles back, Turner and the others watched from the tour van. He removed his pistol from a backpack and chambered a round... just in case.

The tanker pulled to the side of the road and a police officer climbed up the ladder on the side of the tanker. He opened the access hatch on top of the tanker and looked inside. It was filled to capacity with milk. Satisfied, he closed the hatch and climbed down. The tanker was waved through the roadblock and drove down the autobahn.

Turner lowered the gun's hammer and slipped the pistol back into the backpack. Two police officers did a quick check of the tour van and waved it through the roadblock. Turner closed his eyes. He knew he had better get some sleep now, before the next rendezvous point.

Lowell pulled the Mercedes into a gas station and told the island attendant to fill it up. Lowell got out and locked the door. He didn't have time to steal another car and besides, the Mercedes was growing on him. It wasn't a pickup truck, but its ride was a hell of a lot smoother.

He walked into the station's convenience store. He hit the toilet to relieve himself and change his bandages. The bleeding on both wounds had stopped and scabs had formed. It was a good sign. He was encouraged and felt stronger.

He exited the toilet and made himself the largest cappuccino the store's coffee machine could brew. He picked up an armful of chips, beef jerky and a couple of German pastries that he had grown to like.

He brought everything to the counter and told the cashier his pump number so he could pay for the gas. He opened his wallet and looked inside. He was running low on cash, but he didn't dare use his credit or ATM cards. He pushed the pastries and the chips aside but kept the beef jerky and cappuccino. Lowell could live off beef jerky and coffee if he had to and it was looking like he had to. He paid the cashier and asked if she spoke English. She did. "Where is the industrial section of town?" he said.

"We don't have an industrial section," she said. "Not since Volkswagen shut down its transmission plant twenty years ago."

"Where is that... the plant they shut down?"

She gave him directions. He said his thanks, collected his change, jerky, and coffee and exited the store.

He showed the island attendant his receipt verifying that he had paid for the gas and drove off in the direction the cashier had indicated.

Lowell had just finished his coffee when he pulled to a stop in front of the chain link fence that surrounded the abandoned factory. He pulled out Butler's pistol, chambered a round and climbed out of the Mercedes.

He walked to the gate and examined the lock. It had recently been cut open with a bolt cutter. He opened the gate and walked inside the perimeter fence.

Holding the pistol at the ready, he entered the warehouse. He checked to ensure he was alone. He was. He slid his pistol in the back of his pants under his belt and covered it with the tail of his shirt. He saw the railroad tracks and moved to investigate. He knelt down to take a closer look. They were rusty, but some of the steel was exposed meaning that they had been used recently. He followed them to the roll-up door, opened the door using the chain and walked outside.

He followed the rails to the switch and the main train tracks. He tried to rebuild what had happened based on what he could see. Near as he could figure, a freight car or flat car had been loaded in the warehouse and transferred out to a train on the main track.

Lowell walked back inside the warehouse and looked around. He found several sections of pipe that had been recently cut. He found the drum used to burn the mobile phones and the spent phosphorous grenade inside sitting on top of a hardened pool of plastic, mini motherboards and LCD screens from the melted phones. He also found the stubs of several spent welding rods that the technicians had used to seal up the back of the milk tanker truck. But the most telling of evidence was an empty MRE package – beef and cheese lasagna – that had been left by accident between two pieces of machinery. *They were here,* he thought.

Then he heard the sound of a car engine in the front of the warehouse. He pulled out his pistol and hid behind a dilapidated conveyer belt.

Outside the fence, Billy stepped from his rental car parked next to the Mercedes. The driver was nowhere in sight, but Billy suspected he was inside the warehouse, since the gate was open. He wondered if leaving the Lieutenant with her sidearm behind was such a good idea. He passed through the open gate and walked into the abandoned warehouse keeping a cautious eye out for the Mercedes' driver.

Inside the building, Billy had walked halfway into the main part of the warehouse when Lowell stepped out from behind the machinery and said, "What in the hell are you doing here?"

"Good to see you too, Lowell," said Billy.

"Answer my damn question, Smartass," said Lowell.

"I'm looking for you."

"Who's with you?"

"No one. I'm alone."

"Are you sure?"

"Yeah, I'm sure. Are you planning on using that?" said Billy motioning to the pistol.

"I ain't sure yet," said Lowell tucking the gun into the back of his pants.

"What in the hell have you gotten yourself into, Lowell?"

"I don't know. But the water's riding high."

"That's for damn sure. Was he here?"

"Was who here?"

"Turner."

"How do you know about Turner?"

"The Lieutenant that's looking to throw your ass in the brig told me. They think you're in on it. They think you stole Thunder."

"I wouldn't do that. I wouldn't betray my country."

"I know you wouldn't and I told 'em."

"Do any good?"

"Not a damn bit."

"Sounds about right. Yeah, Turner was here. But he ain't now."

"You find anything that might indicate where he's heading?"

"They were working on something. Welding and cutting. I think they used a railcar to transport Thunder."

"It wasn't Thunder. It was ammunition and weapons they stole from the base armory. We found 'em in Pilsen selling the stuff to an arms dealer."

"You found Turner?"

"No. A sergeant named Esposito and mercenary named Laurent."

"Don't know Laurent. But I know Esposito."

"Knew. He's dead."

"Well, that's a shame."

"Yeah. I was hoping he could tell us something, but he chose the hard way."

"I hope the bastard burns in hell."

"Based on the little time I got to know him, I'd say you'd probably get your wish."

"Why the hell would they sell arms and ammunition when they had Thunder?"

"Good question."

"A dime waiting on a dollar."

"That's what I said. It don't make sense. Is that your Mercedes out front?"

"Nah. It's a loaner. I borrowed it."

"You mean you stole it?"

"No. I mean I borrowed it. I'll give it back when I'm done."

"That's the same as stealing, Lowell."

"Is not, penis-breath."

"Watch your mouth, Lowell," said Billy walking up to Lowell and pushing his finger into his chest, "I ain't a kid anymore and I ain't in the mood to put up with your shit."

"Damn it, Billy," said Lowell, grabbing his chest.

"What's wrong?" said Billy panicking.

"Turner shot me."

"You've been shot?!"

"That's what I just said, Piss-bucket."

Billy bit his tongue and said, "Let me see the wound."

"Fuck off."

"Don't be bullheaded and let me see."

Lowell relented and opened his jacket to reveal the big spot of blood on his shirt. "Holy shit, Lowell," said Billy.

"Relax. It's dried. Or at least it was until you poked me."

"I'm sorry. I didn't know."

"It ain't nothing."

"Ain't nothing? You've been shot in the chest."

"I know, Billy. I'm the one that got shot."

"We gotta get you to a hospital."

"I ain't going to no hospital nor doctor either. I took care of it."

"The supplies you stole from the veterinary clinic?"

"Borrowed."

"You ain't a horse, Lowell."

"Same medicine we use, just more of it. I'll be fine as long as you don't poke me again. I think you knocked one of the staples lose."

"Put your hands where I can see 'em. Both of you."

Billy and Lowell turned to see Tien standing at the entrance to the warehouse with her Beretta drawn and leveled at them. They raised their hands. "God damn you, Billy."

"I didn't know, Lowell. She must have followed me."

"Bullshit. You set me up."

"Shut up, Sergeant," said Tien as she moved closer and pulled out her handcuffs.

"Kneel, Sergeant," she said moving up behind Lowell.

Lowell knelt. She put the cuffs on and searched him, removing Butler's pistol from his belt. "You're under arrest, Staff Sergeant Gamble," said Tien.

"I didn't do it, Lieutenant."

"Tell it to your lawyer, Sergeant. Is there anyone else here?"

"No," said Lowell. "It's clear."

"Where's Thunder?"

"Like I said. I wasn't in on it. I have no idea where it's at."

"How about Turner?"

"You really don't listen too good, do ya, Lieutenant? I don't know where Turner is. I don't know where Thunder is. I wasn't in on it."

"Someone gets killed with that weapon system, you'll be charged with murder. So, whatever you do know, I suggest you tell me now."

"I don't know anything."

"That's unfortunate, Sergeant. You could've really helped yourself out."

"He's telling the truth, Lieutenant," said Billy, his hands in the air.

"Billy, can I trust you not to be a problem or do I need to cuff on you too?"

"Cuffs would probably be a good idea. I'm pretty pissed at you right now."

"Have it your way," said Tien pulling a black tie from her pocket, slipping it over Billy's hands and cinching his wrists together. "You two take a seat, back to back."

Billy and Lowell sat back to back. Tien took out another tie and used it to link Lowell's cuffs and Billy's tie. "If you guys decide to run, I will shoot you."

"Wait a minute. I didn't do anything," said Billy.

"Okay. I'll shoot the sergeant twice. Now, sit still and shut up while I have a look around," said Tien moving off.

"Are all the lieutenants that ornery?" said Billy.

"Shut up, asshole," said Lowell.

"Lowell, I didn't know she was following me."

"Don't matter. You led her right to me, ya shithead. You're just lucky I'm in cuffs or I'd beat the ever living shit out of ya."

"You and whose army?" said Billy.

Lowell grabbed one of Billy's fingers and put it in a painful lock using his thumb. "God damn it, Lowell," said Billy.

"Don't need no army to beat you, little brother."

"All right, fine. You win. You're better. You were always better. You were always tougher. There. You happy?"

"Damn right," said Lowell releasing Billy's finger. "Where the hell have you been anyway?"

"What do you mean?" said Billy.

"You disappeared after Pa's funeral. Haven't heard from ya."

"Didn't know you wanted to hear from me."

"You're family. I ain't got no choice in the matter."

Billy was shocked to hear Lowell admit that he cared about him. They both grew silent.

Tien found the empty oil drum and tipped it over. The spent phosphorous grenade rolled out, along with a disk of electronic parts melted together with plastic from the phones. She looked through the parts to see if anything still might work and give her a clue. It was useless. The grenade had done its work well. She moved on, searching…

"I may have something," said Lowell.

"What do you mean?" said Billy.

"After I got shot, I killed the two MPs that was supposed to bury me. I found something in the pockets of their uniforms."

"What?"

"A list of numbers and letters, plus plastic rulers like you'd find at a five and dime. Non-military issue. Something they were probably given. I also found three pieces of a map book."

"You think the list maybe coordinates?"

"I doubt it. The strings are too long to be map coordinates. I was thinking maybe bank account numbers or something like that. I'm not good with puzzles and shit. That's your wheelhouse."

"So, where are they? The lists?"

"Backseat of the Mercedes in a rucksack."

"You're not gonna tell the Lieutenant?"

"Fuck her. I found 'em."

"Lowell, she's got ya dead to rights. Ya gotta do something or you're gonna end up in the brig."

"I ain't afraid of the brig."

"God, you're so bullheaded, you'd rather get locked up than share information?"

"Yeah. It's the only way I can get out of this mess. Find Turner and get Thunder back."

"It's not the only way, Lowell."

"Says you?"

"Yeah. Says me."

Tien walked back over. "Find anything, L.T.?" said Lowell.

"Shut up, Staff Sergeant," said Tien.

"Lieutenant, I'd like the cuffs off now."

"Are you gonna behave?"

"Yes, Lieutenant."

"Pussy," said Lowell.

"I said shut up, Staff Sergeant. You don't want to add disobeying an order from a superior officer to your charges do you?"

"Not sure it's gonna make much difference."

"Okay. I'm sure I can find something to gag you with. Oily rag, maybe someone's used underwear…"

"I'll shut up."

"Good. Stay put and keep your mouth shut and you and I will get along just fine," said Tien pulling out her pocket knife and cutting Billy loose. "Lieutenant, can I have a word… in private?"

"What the fuck are doing, Billy?" said Lowell.

"Saving your ass, big brother," said Billy.

"God damn it, Billy," said Lowell.

"I'm looking for that used underwear, Staff Sergeant," said Tien moving off with Billy out of earshot from Lowell.

"What do you want, Billy?" said Tien.

"A deal."

"What kind of deal?"

"One that gets you Thunder and clears Lowell's name."

"Sounds lovely. How do you propose to do that?"

"I think I can get the location of where they are taking Thunder."

"You think?"

"Yeah. But you gotta let Lowell come with us."

"That ain't happening."

"All right. Let me know if you change your mind."

"If you've got something and you don't share it, I could have you charged with aiding and abetting."

"I'll take that risk."

"Now it's the same for you as it is for Lowell. They kill someone with anything they stole, you could be charged with murder."

"Lieutenant, with all due respect, you're wasting my time and that's a commodity neither of us has right now. I'm gonna find Thunder with or without you. What's it gonna be?"

Tien considered her situation and said, "I suppose, Staff Sergeant Gamble could be an asset when I encounter Thunder. He does know the weapon system better than anyone. But he stays in handcuffs."

"Fine with me. I like him better in handcuffs."

"I'm curious. Why would you trust me again after the exchange at the warehouse?"

"Because I don't have a choice."

"Well, at least I know where I stand," said Tien. "So where's Thunder?"

"I'm gonna need the rucksack from the Mercedes out front."

"All right. Go get what you need. I'll brief Staff Sergeant Gamble on the new terms of his custody."

They both moved off.

"Staff Sergeant Gamble, your brother has convinced me that you should accompany us on our search for Thunder," said Tien.

"How'd he do that?" said Lowell.

"Doesn't matter. What does matter is that you will remain in handcuffs and in my custody. If you run, I will shoot you. Are we clear, Staff Sergeant?"

"Yes, Lieutenant."

"Good. Get your ass up. We're moving out."

"I need to pee first," said Lowell.

"What?"

"I need to urinate. I had a big cup of coffee right before I got here and…"

"Spare me the damn details, Sergeant. Where's the head?"

"Over there, Ma'am," said Lowell motioning with his chin.

They walked over and entered the head. "My hands are cuffed behind my back."

"And they're gonna stay that way."

"Can't get my peter out."

"Peter? What are you… ten?"

"Inches?"

"Years old, Staff Sergeant. Ten years old."

Lowell shrugged. Tien unzipped his trousers and pulled his peter out. "Urinate. That's an order," said Tien. Lowell obeyed.

Billy sat in the Mercedes and opened the rucksack. He pulled out the three map pages, the two lists, and the clear plastic ruler. He looked at the numbers and letters on both lists. They were identical. He looked at the patterns in the sequence of letters and numbers. He noticed the letters were grouped together in two's. That didn't help much in figuring out what they meant, but he found it curious. He studied the map pages. The first page included the location of the meatpacking plant where they found the dead MPs and Lowell was tortured. The second page included the location of the factory where they currently. The third page was a map of Belgium. He picked up the clear plastic ruler and, like Lowell, he placed it on the map in hopes it would reveal something. It didn't.

Tien exited the warehouse with Lowell. "Okay, Billy. Where is Thunder?" said Tien.

"I don't know exactly where it is right now, but it will be in Belgium," said Billy.

"I could've told ya that," said Lowell.

"Shut up, Staff Sergeant. Where in Belgium?"

"I don't know yet. I'm working on it."

"Work faster," said Tien.

"Yeah, Billy. Work faster," said Lowell.

"Zip it, Sergeant," said Tien.

"You already did," said Lowell with a snicker.

"Until I figure out exactly where we are going, we can head to Belgium," said Billy.

"All right. We'll take my car," said Tien.

"Mines more comfortable," said Lowell.
"Yours is stolen," said Billy.
"You stole a Mercedes?" said Tien.
"Borrowed," said Lowell.
"Like I said, we're taking my car," said Tien.

FIFTEEN

Specialist Cox sat working on the HEAT tank round laying on the table in front of him. The High-Explosive Anti-Tank shell used a shaped charge to pierce the outer armor of a tank, then melt the inner layer of steel inside the tank sending a jet of molten metal into the crew compartment. It was very effective against medium tanks and armored troop carriers, but could not penetrate the composite armor of late-model main battle tanks. That was the sabot shell's job.

The U.S. Army had designed a safety feature that only armed the tank shell after it had achieved a preset distance from the tank's barrel. This delay feature prevented a shell from exploding too close to the barrel and killing the crew that launched it. Turner and his team had a use for the shells that required it to explode shortly after being fired, so the delay feature had to be altered in each shell to zero distance. It was a long and tedious procedure that requires each shell casing to be opened and again sealed close. Once the delay feature was defeated, the round became live and would explode when the tip of the shell came in contact with a hard object making it much more dangerous to handle.

Cox didn't trust the other technicians to alter the shells. If they failed to execute the procedure correctly the shell could explode, killing the technician and everyone else in the immediate vicinity. An improperly executed procedure could also render the shell useless and unable to accomplish its task. It was better to do it himself, he thought. He had a lot riding on the success of the mission and even more riding on its failure. Once he had crossed the line between professional soldier and criminal there was no turning back. Getting caught meant life in prison… a military prison. Failure was not an option he cared to entertain.

He had been at work altering the shells for almost five hours without a break. Master Sergeant Turner was not a man he wanted to piss off by falling behind his precious schedule. He could see the tremors in his fingers increasing the longer he used them for the meticulous job which required using a soldering gun around high-explosives. *OSHA would have a fit,* he thought and laughed to himself.

Back on the streets of Belgium, a water utility van pulled up in front of a manhole cover on a busy downtown street and parked, blocking traffic. Visser, now wearing a hardhat, water company overalls and a utility tool belt, stepped from the van, moved to the back and opened the rear doors. He pulled out orange safety cones and placed them in back of the van to divert traffic. He placed a small utility fence around the manhole cover to prevent anyone from falling into the manhole once it was open and to prevent anyone from seeing what he was doing. He removed a five-gallon plastic bucket filled with tools and supplies from the back of the van and placed it next to the manhole cover.

He knelt down and studied the gap between the manhole cover and the steel rim of the manhole. He reached into his utility belt and pulled out a mix of metal washers. He placed the washers in a stack trying different thickness of washers until he found the correct combination to slide into the gap. He removed the stack of washers and placed them on the pavement beside the manhole. He added one thin washer to the stack making it slightly thicker than the gap. He pulled out a tube of Super Glue from his utility belt and placed several drops of adhesive between each of the washers and let it dry until the stack felt solid.

He placed the hook under the edge of the manhole cover and removed it, sliding it to one side of the exposed manhole. Then he used a cloth soaked in industrial strength cleaning solution to wipe around the edges of the manhole cover and the manhole rim. He tied a rope around the handle of the bucket and lowered it into the hole. He slipped a flashlight onto his helmet and turned it on. He pulled out his mobile phone and dialed. A man answered. "Standby," said Visser and hung up the phone. He dialed another number and said the same thing before hanging up.

He slipped the phone back into his pocket and climbed down into the manhole.

Below the manhole was a chamber encased in concrete. He reached the bottom of the ladder and looked around. There were several utility conduits and a thirty-two-inch diameter steel pipe running under the street – the water main. In the middle of the pipe was a shutoff valve. He turned the wheel on the valve until the water was shut off. He pulled an insulated can of liquid nitrogen from the bucket and sprayed the wheel shaft for over a minute until it was frosted. He lifted a sledgehammer from the bucket and struck the side of the wheel repeatedly. On the forth whack, the iron shaft broke off and the wheel fell to the concrete floor making the valve inoperable and difficult to replace. He climbed back up the ladder and sat on the edge of the manhole as he dialed his mobile again. The man answered. "Go," said Visser and hung up. He dialed again and another man answered. "Go," said Visser again and hung up.

Several blocks away, in the basement of the office building, the thirty-two-inch steel water pipe had been exposed through the new hole in the basement wall and excavated so that it could be accessed from all sides. De Jong hung up his phone and started the timer on his watch. He nodded to Meijer standing beside the main line wearing safety goggles and holding a portable gas-powered circular saw with a diamond blade. Meijer started the saw's engine and went to work. Spark flew as he cut along the chalk markings on the pipe, now empty of water.

Back on the street, Visser lifted himself out of the manhole and used the rope to bring the bucket back up. He pushed the manhole cover back over the hole until it thumped into place. He again lifted the manhole cover with the cover hook until it was ajar three-inches. He placed the stack of washers just inside the manhole rim and lowered the manhole cover until the stack of washers was wedged between the rim and the cover. He removed the hook allowing the cover to be supported at an angle by the stack of washers. He pulled the sledgehammer from the bucket and whacked the manhole cover until it was once again flush with the rim. The stack of washers was compressed inside the gap. He pulled a two-sided cartridge of epoxy and accelerator held in its dual applicator from the bucket and applied a thick bead of adhesive into the gap around the edge of the manhole. He used a portable blowtorch to dry the adhesive in place. He placed the hook into the gap beside the stack of washers and tried to pry open the manhole cover. It didn't budge. Satisfied, he stepped into the van and drove away leaving the supplies and tools in the street.

A few minutes later, the real water company repairmen arrived to inspect the water main valve after having received multiple complaints of no water. Unable to open the manhole cover, they were forced to call in a welder with an acetylene cutting torch to cut the manhole open. It would take another five hours to shut off the water from the local pumping station, then replace the wheel and shaft on the main line valve. That was all the time Visser and his teams required.

Meijer finished cutting both ends of a large section of pipe out of the water main. De Jong helped him move it out of the way and checked his watch. "How are we doing on time?" said Meijer.

"It's gonna be tight. Let's keep moving," said De Jong.

Meijer and De Jong used a portable pneumatic jack to roll and raise the access pipe section into place lining up the two ends with the main line. De Jong slipped on a face shield and heavy gloves. He connected the clamp of an arc welder cable to the bare metal on a valve on the access chamber. He placed a welding rod in the other clamp connected by a cable to the arc welder. He lowered his face shield and went to work welding together the two ends of the new pipe section to the main line.

Once De Jong finished the last weld on the outside of the pipe segment, he opened the main valve and the access hatch. He climbed inside the pipe and welded the seams on the inside of the pipe ensuring that it was completely waterproof.

De Jong finished welding the new pipe section to the main line. He climbed out of the access hatch and closed it. Meijer opened the valve and peered into the chamber's glass portal. As expected, nothing happened. There was still no water in the main line. They sat down and waited while eating their lunch.

After forty minutes the portal showed that water was once again filling the main line. De Jong checked for leaks around his welds. There were none. He closed the shutoff valve. Meijer waited until the water had receded in the portal and opened the access hatch to the chamber. He turned on a flashlight and looked inside the chamber. He could see thirty feet down the inside of the empty mainline. The inside of the pipe was smooth. He pulled his head out of the chamber and closed the access hatch. De Jong opened the valve and the chamber once again filled with water. Meijer wheeled a portable gas-powered pump next to the mainline. He connected a short section of fireman's hose from one of the Storz couplers on the new pipe section to the portable pump and opened the valve to the coupler. Water gushed out of the opposite side of the pump. Meijer started the pump's engine and water pressure increased three times. He shut down the engine and closed the valve. "Looks like we're good to go," said Meijer.

De Jong called Visser on his mobile and said, "We are operational."

Tien drove. Lowell rode in the front passenger seat where she could keep an eye on him, and Billy sat in the backseat studying the three maps. "We're coming up on the Belgian border. Do you have a location yet?" said Tien.

"If I did you'd be the first to know," said Billy.

"That's not helpful," she said.

"I'm doing the best I can."

"Do it faster. We're kinda on the clock here."

"That's not helpful," said Billy. "Maybe we can narrow down the possible locations."

"How's that?" said Tien.

"If they were going to sell it they probably would have moved it East toward Russia or South toward the Middle East. That's where the buyers would be, right?"

"Most of the buyers, yes."

"What do you mean 'most'?"

"Terrorists can be located anywhere."

"Plus, Thunder has a small footprint and is lightweight when compared to a tank. It could be flown out of almost any airport that can support a heavy lift cargo plane. Hell, it could even be lifted with a helicopter." said Lowell.

"And let's not forgot cargo ships. Belgium has a major port in Antwerp," said Tien. "Brussels is also a rail hub. Thunder could easily be loaded on a flatcar and transported just about anywhere. Just because they are rendezvousing in Belgium, doesn't mean that's the weapon's final destination."

"Okay, fine. Humor me and let's go down the path of terrorists. There's only so many things you can do with it. I mean, it's military hardware, right?" said Billy.

"Okay. Lowell, you're the expert. What are its capabilities?" said Tien.

"Well. It's good at destroying tanks that's for damn sure," said Lowell.

"Are there a lot of tanks in Belgium?" said Billy.

"No. Belgians ain't got any tanks. They do have quite a few armored personnel carriers. But using Thunder on an APC is like using a shotgun on a field mouse. Complete overkill," said Lowell.

"So, how else could they use it?"

"It's basically a mobile cannon with a minigun kicker. It can destroy just about anything or anyone," said Lowell.

"So, assassination is a possibility?" said Tien.

"Again, complete overkill, but yeah, I suppose they could use it for an assassination. I'd say it's more likely they'd use it as a weapon of mass destruction. It's really the perfect weapon for a terrorist that wants to kill a lot of civilians," said Lowell.

"What about a building like a skyscraper?" said Billy.

"Piece of cake," said Lowell. "Thunder could roll right up to the front doors and take out the support pillar using HEAT rounds. The shaped charge would melt the rebar inside the concrete casings. The thing would topple over like a drunk longshoreman on Friday night."

"How about a dam?" said Tien.

"I imagine. Be a bit more difficult. They could use a series of sabot rounds to break through the concrete. Then they could switch to HEAT rounds to fracture the structure. It'd take some time, but it'd work. Plus you've got all that water pressure pushing from the opposite side. Yeah, a dam is doable."

"And a nuclear power plant? Belgium's got two," said Billy looking at his smartphone.

"Again, a piece of cake," said Lowell. "Probably only take a couple of sabot rounds to pierce the reactor's outer wall. Follow up with HEAT shot into the core and you'd have yourself a regular Chernobyl."

"That's not very encouraging," said Tien.

"Didn't know I was in charge of morale," said Lowell.

"You're not in charge of anything right now, Staff Sergeant," said Tien.

"And here I thought we were starting to get along so fine."

"You thought wrong," said Tien.

"I suppose we should add the European Union and NATO Headquarters to the list of possible targets. Both are located in Brussels. If you're a terrorist and you want to make headlines, taking down either would make a pretty bold statement," said Billy.

Tien pulled out her mobile phone.

"Who are you calling?" said Billy.

"NATO command. I've got to warn them," she said.

"Lowell, the Lieutenant's got a thing called a Javelin in the trunk. Could that stop Thunder?" said Billy to Lowell in a hushed tone.

"A Javelin? Probably. Thunder ain't got much in the way of armor. It uses speed and maneuverability to keep out of harm's way. The problem ain't destroying it. The problem is finding it. It's got reactive camouflage. Once activated, you could stand twenty-feet away from it and you'd never even know it was there."

"Great," said Billy.

"Yep. Thunder's one hell of a weapon system," said Lowell like a proud father.

The milk tanker and other vehicles drove into an industrial neighborhood and pulled up to the front of a warehouse. A roll-up door opened and the vehicles drove into the building.

The tanker truck drove over to a drain in the concrete floor inside the building. A technician opened the valves on the side of the tanker and thousands of gallons of milk poured out of the couplers into the drain. He climbed up the tanker and opened the access hatch. He looked down as the milk level sank and revealed Thunder hidden inside the tanker.

A flatbed tow truck pulled into the warehouse and parked near the milk tanker. A technician with a portable circular saw finished cutting the back off the milk tanker. The stainless steel oval piece fell away revealing Thunder covered in puddles of milk. "All right. Get it out of there and get it cleaned up. I want it armed and operational in two hours," said Turner to the group of technicians.

A security guard entered the basement of the office building. He checked each of the doors to ensure they were secure.

He saw the large hole in the wall revealing the water main and the access chamber. He moved to investigate. His father had worked for the Water Department, so he was familiar with the water mains that ran below the city streets. In all the years that he had accompanied his father, he had never seen anything that looked like the access chamber, especially with the eight Storz couplers and shutoff valves.

He pulled out his radio to call the building manager. There was a sick thud as a knife blade plunged into his back. The guard fell to the floor dead. Behind him, Visser stood, emotionless. *Wrong place, wrong time,* thought Visser.

Billy, Lowell, and Tien sat in a conference room waiting. Four-Star General Hanson, commander of NATO forces, entered like a man on a mission and wasted no time with chit-chat. His staff, an entourage of generals and colonels, followed. Tien and Lowell snapped to attention and saluted. This was the first time either of them had stood in the same room as a four-star general, let alone the commander of NATO. "At ease," said Hanson. "Why am I talking to you, Lieutenant Tien?"

"Sir, approximately 42 hours ago a DARPA weapon system was hijacked en route to a U.S. Air Force base. We believe it is on its way here to Belgium."

"I have already been briefed on the weapon system and what it is capable of. Why do you believe it is on its way here?"

"General, we discovered three maps in the belongings of an MP that was a suspect in the hijacking."

"Was a suspect?"

"Yes, sir. Staff Sergeant Gamble, the weapon system operator, was kidnapped. He killed the MP while escaping," said Tien motioning to Lowell.

"Well done, Staff Sergeant. Although, it would have been nice if we could have interrogated the son of a bitch," said Hanson.

"Wasn't really an option, General," said Lowell.

"Gonna have to trust you on that one, Staff Sergeant," said Hanson. "You know this weapon?"

"Yes, General," said Lowell. "Like the back of my hand."

"Good to know," said Hanson. "So, these three maps…"

"Yes, General. Two of the maps were areas in Germany where the perpetrators had carried out part of their plan. The third map was of Belgium," said Tien.

"Okay. So where is it?"

"We're working on that too, General," said Billy.

"Who the hell are you?"

"This is Billy Gamble, General. He was sent by the CIA," said Tien.

"CIA?"

"Yes, General," said Billy.

"Mr. Gamble, I hope you don't take offense, but you don't look much like a CIA agent," said Hanson.

"Thank you, General," said Billy. "I'm not. But they use me from time to time to find things or people."

"Who do you report to?"

"His name is Culper," said Billy watching Hanson's expression sharpen.

"I thought he retired," said Hanson.

"As I understand it, he went freelance, General," said Billy. "Kind of a manager of subcontractors."

"You mean 'Mercenaries'?"

"I'm not a mercenary, General," said Billy.

Hanson grunted. He took a moment to consider, then he said, "Okay. Here's what we are going to do and not do. We're not gonna play the blame-game right now, but I can promise you there will be an investigation once we have dealt with the problem at hand," said Hanson.

"Yes, sir," said Tien.

"Lieutenant Tien, you will turn over everything you have to military intelligence and my staff. They'll take it from here."

"Sir?"

"It's pretty simple, Lieutenant. From what I have been told this whole thing was a cluster-fuck from the start and I now have an advanced U.S. Army weapon system running amok someplace in Belgium. You are relieved, Lieutenant. You will make yourself available to answer any questions the new officer in charge has concerning the investigation up to this point. Are we clear?"

"Yes, General," said Tien, stunned.

"Mr. Gamble, you can go back to Culper and tell him I said Thanks, but no thanks. We'll handle this one on our own."

"What about my brother, General?"

"Your brother?"

"Staff Sergeant Gamble," said Billy motioning to Lowell."

"Oh, yeah," said Hanson. "Lieutenant Tien, once you have answered all the questions my staff may have about this investigation you will take Staff Sergeant Gamble back to his base and place him in the brig until the investigation into this hijacking is complete and his participation in said crime has been determined."

"Yes, sir," said Tien.

"I think we are done here," said Hanson and exited leaving his staff to deal with his orders.

Billy, Lowell, and Tien sat in shock. "Lieutenant Tien, you mentioned three map pages and a list retrieved from one of the MPs that kidnapped the Staff Sergeant?" said Hanson's Deputy General.

"Yes, sir. Billy has the lists and the map pages," said Tien. "There's also a rucksack, a web belt and two pistols in the trunk of my car."

Billy reached into his pocket and pulled out the three map pages and one of the two lists. He left the clear plastic ruler and the other list hidden in his pocket. He handed the list and map pages to the general. Tien noticed that Billy was only handing over one of the lists and said, "General?"

"Yes, Lieutenant," said the General.

Tien exchanged a look with Billy. She could see that he was still determined. She turned to the general and said, "Is there anything else you require?"

"We'd like to debrief each of you separately, assuming Mr. Gamble agrees."

"I agree," said Billy.

"Good. Once that is completed you are free to go and Lieutenant Tien you are free to return Staff Sergeant Gamble back to his base."

"Very well, General," said Tien.

Tien pulled the two pistols, WEB belt, and rucksack from the trunk of the rental car and handed them to two MPs. The MPs saluted her and re-entered the building. Tien climbed into the driver's seat of the car where Lowell and Billy were already seated. "Are you out of your fucking mind?" said Tien. "Withholding evidence in a federal investigation is a felony."

"It's a technicality, Lieutenant. The lists were identical. I gave them one. That's all they needed," said Billy.

"Why do you care? It's over," said Tien.

"For you maybe. But I came here to help my brother. The only way I can do that is to find Thunder."

"You heard the general," said Tien.

"Your general has no jurisdiction over me," said Billy. "And if I were you, I might wanna reconsider my involvement in completing your mission."

"I have my orders," said Tien.

"Yeah, ya do," said Billy. "But let me ask you… How is this whole thing gonna play out when it comes to your career? You've just been relieved by a four-star general."

"My career is over," said Tien. "I'll turn in my retirement papers as soon as I return to my base."

"You seem sad about that," said Billy.

"You're damn right I am. I love the service."

"So, you're just gonna let it go without a fight?"

"What options do I have?"

"The only one that I can see is to win," said Billy.

Tien considered and said, "I was ordered to return your brother to his base."

"Yeah, but he didn't give you a deadline. What would an extra twenty-four hours matter? Your ass is grass anyway, right?" said Billy.

"You think we can find Thunder in one day?" said Tien.

"It's possible. The one thing I know for sure is that we ain't gonna find it in this parking lot," said Billy.

"Where to?" said Tien starting the engine.

"I think better when I'm not hungry. I know a good bistro in the old quarter," said Billy.

"You think lunch is gonna help us find Thunder?" said Tien.

"Couldn't hurt," said Billy.

"I am a bit peckish myself," said Lowell.

"Shut up, Staff Sergeant," said Tien as she put the car in gear and drove off.

SIXTEEN

A Mercedes Sprinter van pulled to a stop in front of a Belgian hotel with a large square in front of it. Specialist Cox got out and opened the side and rear doors, revealing a dozen heavy-duty Anvil cases for transporting electronics and a six-foot-tall equipment rack enclosed in dark glass with an air-conditioning unit mounted on top. Several bellhops with luggage carts helped him unload.

With the cases in tow, Cox looked like a roadie for a rock-and-roll band as he approached the front desk. He was greeted in Dutch by the receptionist. He responded in English expecting that she would understand. She did. "I have a reservation under the name Daryl Smith," said Cox.

"Yes, Mr. Smith. We have been expecting you. You have a reservation for a penthouse."

"…facing the square," Cox added.

"Yes, facing the square."

"Will you be joined by others?"

"Nope. Just little old me."

"You look like you're setting up a concert."

"No. Just video games. Can't live without 'em."

"I see," she said, handing the keycard to the lead bellhop. "I hope you enjoy your stay."

"I'm sure I will," said Cox as he turned to follow the bellhop.

Inside the penthouse, Cox moved to the balcony overlooking the square below. It was a wide view, unobstructed. He moved back inside, tipped the bellhop and closed the door. He rolled up his sleeves and unpacked the shipping cases.

Inside the cases were the individual pieces of the Thunder control console. He slid the electronics into the air-conditioned rack and attached dozens of cables to the leads in the back of the electronics like a rat's nest of wires. He knew every connection by memory. He had practiced setting it up over a dozen times until he no longer needed the wiring diagrams. He was confident when he finally pressed the power button it would all work flawlessly.

He set up the console and video monitors on multiple portable tables by the balcony window. He moved an overstuffed chair up to the tables and sat down. It was a little lower than what he liked, but it would do. He pulled out a belt holster holding his pistol from behind his back. He taped the holster to the bottom of the chair. He wasn't expecting to be disturbed, but one could never be too cautious, he thought.

He rearranged the equipment until he was satisfied with its placement and feel. He had a three-hundred and sixty-degree view using the video screens.

Cox carried several cases up a flight of stairs and through a doorway that accessed the roof of the hotel. He moved to the edge of the roof at the front of the hotel so that he could see the square below. He opened the cases and remove a portable microwave antenna array. He set the device up on a beefy tripod. He attached a cable harness to the device and lowered the cable on to the penthouse balcony below. He hid the shipping cases behind an air-conditioning unit and left the rooftop.

Cox reentered the penthouse and retrieved the cable harness from the balcony. He connected the harness to the equipment in the rack and tested the signal. It worked exactly as planned. The signal was strong.

Room service brought him a bucket of iced beer, a cheeseburger and a basket of Belgium fries with mayonnaise. He munched and drank the first two bottles of beer while testing his gear. He knew the system's idiosyncrasies and how to quickly repair any problem. He popped a couple of fries in his mouth and leaned back in the chair, confident and ready to go to war.

Cox was young and his mind was sharp. He grew up with video games and felt most at home sitting behind a stack of high definition monitors holding a joystick like the one used to operate Thunder. His reaction time and his manual dexterity were excellent. Cox was the new warrior trained to fight the enemies of the 21st Century with technology. He was anxious for his chance to prove himself worthy. He thought of Master Sergeant Turner like the father he never had, and he had been honored when Turner asked him to become part of his team and operate Thunder. He would do whatever it took to impress Turner and make him proud.

Lowell and Tien finished their meal as Billy finished the last fries in a basket while studying the list of numbers and letters. "Why write it by hand?" said Billy thinking out loud.

"Maybe they were in a hurry?" said Lowell.

"Maybe," said Billy. "But the way they're written… It's strange. Some of the characters are perfectly formed, while others seem to be scribbled, plus the spacing is all off. It's almost like…" Billy stopped mid-sentence, thinking…

"It's almost like what?" said Tien.

Billy pulled the clear plastic ruler from his pocket and set on the list. He lined the first-centimeter mark on the ruler with the first character on the list. The perfectly formed letters lined up with each centimeter mark. "I'll be damned," said Lowell watching.

Lowell reached for a napkin and grabbed a pen from Tien's pocket. "What the hell you think you're doing, Staff Sergeant?" said Tien.

"Shoot," said Lowell to Billy.

Billy called out each of the characters under the centimeter marks while Lowell transcribed on to the napkin. There were three strings of characters. Each string was divided into two sections. When Billy finished, Lowell looked down at what he had written, smiled and said, "They're map coordinates."

"Are you sure?" said Tien.

"I drive tanks for a living, Ma'am. I'm sure," said Lowell. "We need a map book."

"There's a bookstore across the square," said Billy.

"No, go. That's gonna be civilian shit. We need a NATO map book," said Lowell.

Tien drove up to the guard gate outside USAG Benelux - a U.S. military base on the Northeastern side of Brussels. She showed her military I.D. and said, "Where are the MPs posted?"

The guard gave her directions and waved her through. She drove onto the base.

Tien entered the MPs office and approached the receptionist. The receptionist, a young private, saluted and said, "How can I help you, Lieutenant?"

"I need a NATO map book," said Tien.

Tien drove to a park near the base and parked the car. She got out and walked over to Billy and Lowell, sitting with their backs to a tree, their hands cuffed together with plastic wrap ties. "You get it?" said Billy.

"Mission accomplished," said Tien pulling a pocket knife from her pocket and cutting the ties on their wrists.

"Not sure why you needed to handcuff me too," said Billy.

"I didn't want you helping him," said Tien as she put a pair of handcuffs back on Lowell.

"I ain't going anywhere, L.T.," said Lowell. "I want to see this thing through just as much as you do. More in fact."

"If I remove your handcuff and you run, I will be forced to shoot you," said Tien.

"Roger that," said Lowell.

"I have your word you'll behave and go back to your base with me once we find Thunder?"

"You have my word."

"Is his word good?" said Tien to Billy.

"Yeah, it's good," said Billy.

Tien removed the handcuffs and handed Lowell the NATO map book. Billy read the first set of coordinates. Lowell looked up the location and said "It checks out. It's the location of the hijacking."

Billy read off the second set of coordinates. Lowell flipped through the map books pages until he found the correct location and said, "Still good. It's location of the abandoned factory near Frankfurt."

Billy read off the third set of coordinates. Lowell looked them up in the book. "Antwerp," said Lowell.

"Antwerp?" said Tien.

"That's what it says," said Lowell. "Looks like it could be an industrial neighborhood near the harbor judging by the spacing of the buildings."

"That would make sense if they were going to load it on a ship," said Tien.

"The NATO MPs took my pistols. We might consider picking up some more firepower before we go up against Turner and his team," said Lowell. "They're playing for keeps."

"Belgian gun laws are tough. It would take too long to buy a firearm through a legitimate dealer," said Billy. "We could try the black market."

"No. We're in enough potential trouble as it. We don't need to get caught with black market weapons by the Belgian police," said Tien. "We recon the building, find Thunder and notify the military. We let them take down Turner and his team."

"And what happens if we run into Turner or his men before the military gets there?" said Lowell.

"I've still got my sidearm. I'll protect you," said Tien.

Lowell and Billy exchange a dubious look.

Visser walked into a garden square with food kiosks around the edges. He ordered a pastry from one of the stands and sat down at a table across from Jacob Lund, drinking a coffee. They spoke in Dutch. "Do you have it?" said Visser.

Lund placed a memory stick on the table beside his coffee. Visser reached for it. Lund placed his hand over it and said, "Funds transfer first."

"All right. But so we are clear… if the information does not work to our satisfaction, the individual I work for is very good at finding people."

"The information is correct. I was on the design team for the entire facility."

"And the soft points?"

"They are on overlays. You'll see them when you open the schematic."

"Schematic. There's only one?"

"All eight were designed using the same equipment. You only need one schematic."

"And yet you charged me one hundred thousand for each."

"I charged eight hundred thousand for the risk I am taking, which is substantial. Are we doing business or not?"

Visser pulled out his smartphone and sent a text message. He set his phone down and took a bite of his pastry. "Delicious," said Visser.

"Fuck this. I'm not playing games," said Lund and rose from the table.

"Relax. It takes a minute or two for the funds transfer to go through," said Visser.

Lund sat back down and pulled out his smartphone. He opened a bank app and looked up his account. The balance changed from a few thousand euro to over eight hundred thousand. Lund slid the memory stick over to Visser. "You'll need the password to unlock the files," said Lund.

"And what might that be?"

"Two words with an underscore between them - Market Garden."

Visser chuckled and said, "I hope we have more luck than the Allies."

"Yes, but if you don't... and any of this comes back to me, you'll be the one with the problem," said Lund. "I know people too."

"Of course," said Visser, rising from the table and walking away as he slipped the memory stick into his pocket.

Cox answered a knock on his hotel room door. It was Visser. "You got it?" said Cox.

Visser handed him the memory stick and gave him the password. Cox walked over to the computer console and inserted the memory stick. He punched in several commands on the computer's keyboard and a schematic appeared on the monitors. "Nice," said Cox. "Are you sure it's accurate?"

"He understood the consequences if it was not and seemed unworried," said Visser.

"And the soft points?"

"There should be an overlay."

Cox punched in several more commands and the overlay appeared on the schematic. "Excellent," said Cox.

"So we are good?" said Visser.

"Good?" said Cox with a smile. "We are golden."

Tien parked in an industrial area of Antwerp. "The building's around the next corner. We'll approach on foot," said Tien.

They got out of the vehicle. Tien opened the trunk and pulled out her WEB belt holding her pistol and extra ammunition. "Maybe we should take Javelin?" said Lowell.

"We're not looking for a firefight," said Tien. "Recon only, remember?"

"Ain't like I got much say in the matter," said Lowell.

"No. You don't, Staff Sergeant," said Tien. "You're welcome to wait in the trunk of the car."

"Not hardly," said Lowell.

"Let's move," said Tien.

They walked to the corner of the block. Tien peeked around the edge of a building. "Looks like we may have the right place. They've got two men in plain clothes posted out front. No weapons that I could see, but I don't imagine they'd want the attention if a police car happened to pass by."

"Are you gonna call the military for backup?" said Billy.

"Not this time. Not until I see Thunder with my own eyes," said Tien.

"How are we supposed to get past their lookouts?" said Billy.

"We go up. The neighboring buildings' rooftops are close enough together we should be able to jump across and gain access," said Tien.

"Not a bad plan, L.T.," said Lowell. "You think they might have thought the same thing and posted a lookout on the roof?"

"Yes. So, let's be real quiet," said Tien.

"Roger that," said Lowell.

Billy picked up a broken brick from the street gutter.

"What's that for?" said Tien.

"Plan B," said Billy.

They maneuvered through a series of side streets and alleyways until they came to the back of the adjacent building. Billy found an open emergency door on the side of the building.

They entered, found the stairwell leading to the roof and started to climb.

They moved out on to the rooftop and kept low, out of sight from the target building's rooftop. They moved to the edge and Tien peeked over the lip. "One guard, armed with a submachine gun, near the rooftop doorway," said Tien.

Billy took a peek over the edge.

"You don't trust me?" said Tien, incredulous.

"It's not that. I was just getting my bearings," said Billy.

"Okay. So, here's the plan," said Tien. "Staff Sergeant, you create a diversion to lure the lookout over to —"

Without warning, Billy popped up and threw the half-a-brick like a baseball hitting the lookout in the head. He crumpled to the rooftop. "What the hell was that?" said Tien.

"Plan B," said Billy.

"You're not much for following orders, are you?" said Tien.

"No. I'm not," said Billy.

"He's really not," said Lowell.

They moved across the rooftops. Tien knelt down to check the lookout's pulse and said, "He's still alive."

"That's unfortunate," said Lowell, picking up the lookout's submachine gun. He pulled the guard's mobile and extra ammunition clips from his pockets.

Tien pulled out a plastic tie and cuffed the lookout's hands behind his back. She took another tie and secured his hands around a pipe leading to a water storage tank. "That'll hold him for a while," said Tien. "Let's go."

As they moved toward the rooftop doorway, Billy looked over at the unconscious lookout and saw a bulge in his jacket pocket. He knelt down and removed a grenade and a pocket knife from the man's pocket and slipped it into his own. They entered the rooftop doorway and walked down the stairwell.

At the bottom of the stairwell was a door. They moved through it and into a hallway with doors on both sides. "Staff Sergeant, you check right, I'll check left," said Tien.

Lowell nodded. They opened each door and moved inside each room checking it for occupants. Billy trailed behind keeping watch on the hallway. He wasn't exactly sure what he could do with only a knife and a hand grenade, but he figured somebody should keep watch while Lowell and Tien searched the rooms. The rooms were empty like the place had been abandoned.

Tien came to the men's bathroom. She moved inside and checked the stalls. Nobody was inside.

Lowell came to the woman's bathroom and moved inside. He moved toward the stalls when he heard a toilet flush. He readied his submachine gun. A stall door opened and a woman walked out tucking in her blouse. It was Garza. "L.T.?" said Lowell stunned to see her.

"Oh my god, you're alive," said Garza moving up to him, wrapping her arms around his neck and hugging him. "I saw Turner shoot you."

"Yeah, well... I guess I'm tougher than I look. What are you doing here? How did you escape?"

"I didn't. They're still here."

Lowell turned back to the doorway and said, "You stay here. I've got to warn the others."

"The others?"

"Yeah. My brother Billy and a Lieutenant. We've been hunting for you and Thunder. Wait here. I'll just be a minute," said Lowell moving toward the door.

Lowell stopped when he heard a familiar noise – the cock of a pistol trigger. He had heard the sound a thousand times before at the military shooting ranges and at home on the ranch when his father would take Billy and he out shooting. He turned back toward Garza and saw her pointing a 9mm Beretta at his face, "You should have joined us, Lowell. It would have made things so much easier. He's got this thing ratcheted down to the last detail. He thought of everything," said Garza.

"Turner?" said Lowell.

"Turner is smart and a warrior, but he's not capable of planning something this complex," said

Garza taking final aim with the pistol. "Sorry, it had to end this way, Lowell. You were one hell of a lay."

Garza hesitated for a moment when she caught a glimpse of somebody else moving through the doorway into the bathroom. It was Billy diving to the floor and throwing the pocket knife he had found on the rooftop lockout. It was one hell of a throw considering he was moving when the knife left his hand. It hit Garza in the chest. She never realized what had happened. There was no blood pumping to her brain. The knife's blade had entered her heart and cut the main artery. She collapsed without firing a shot and died.

Lowell was in shock. He had lost her again. Rage filled him and he released it the way he always had in the past... on Billy. He jumped on top of his brother, hit him several times in the face and put his hands around his neck. Billy chocked, unable to breathe. He punched Lowell in the ribs hoping to break his hold. It didn't. It was Tien's pistol pressing against the back of his head and her words that finally made him release Billy, "Let go of him, Staff Sergeant. He had no choice. He's your brother for God's sake."

Lowell let up his grip and rolled off Billy. She was right. Billy had no choice. Billy hacked and coughed until air was once again flowing into his lungs. Tien walked over to Garza and checked her pulse. She was dead. Tien picked up her pistol and handed it to Billy. "They're here someplace. Let's keep moving," said Tien moving back into the hallway.

Billy looked over at Lowell. His chest wound was bleeding again. "I think you popped a staple or two," said Billy.

"I don't give a shit," said Lowell.

"Yeah... but I do," said Billy moving to his side and opening his shirt to examine the wound.

"Leave it. I've lived through worse," said Lowell.

"Yeah. You have," said Billy. "I'll check it later, once we're done clearing the building. Okay?"

Lowell nodded. Billy rose and offered Lowell a hand up. Lowell took it. It occurred to Billy that this was the first time in his life that Lowell had ever accepted his help. He wanted to say something but decided to just let the moment pass. It was what it was - one brother helping another. No words were necessary.

Billy and Lowell moved back into the hallway. Tien stood near the end of the hallway. She turned back and waved them forward, motioning for them to keep quiet. As Billy and Lowell approached, they heard voices coming from an office doorway at the end of a hallway. All three moved up to the outside of the doorway. Tien was the first to move inside. Lowell followed.

The room was vacant. The voices were coming through an open window in the walls. The room was the payroll department office where the workers would collect their checks through a window leading into the warehouse. On one side of the office was an old steel safe used to hold cash before checks became popular. There were several old heavy-duty office desks covered in dust. They knelt down behind the desks as they peered into the warehouse through the window.

SEVENTEEN

The MPs, engineers, and technicians, now wearing body armor, were busy loading up several trucks and cars with crates of military supplies and gear stolen from the armory. Thunder sat under a tarp on the back of the flatbed tow truck. Turner was nearby on his phone. "Specialist Cox, are you operational?" said Turner into the phone.

"Up and running, Master Sergeant," said Cox.

"Outstanding," said Turner. "Sit tight. We are on our way. From here on out we communicate through radio until the operation is finished."

"Wilco, Master Sergeant," said Cox.

Turner hung up and moved toward the tow truck. "Load up. I want everyone ready to move in three minutes," said Turner to his men in the warehouse.

The team members climbed into several civilian vehicles including two delivery trucks. An MP climbed into the tow truck's driver seat. Turner called the two lookouts in the front of the building and ordered them to load up. They entered the warehouse and climbed into one of the vehicles. Turner dialed the number for the lookout on the roof.

The rooftop lookout's phone rang in Lowell's pocket. Lowell, Billy, and Tien all hit the floor behind the desks. Lowell fumbled for the phone.

Turner heard the phone ringing and turned toward the payroll office. "Simpson, what the fuck are you doing? You're supposed to be on watch on the roof," said Turner staring at the empty window, the phone still ringing.

Lowell pressed 'ignore' and the phone stopped ringing.

Turner looked at his mobile and saw that the call was disconnected. "Simpson?" he said again.

There was no response. Turner took a moment to consider. He pulled out his knife, opened the blade and walked along the back of the tow truck cutting the rope that held the tarp in place. He slipped on his radio headset and said, "Red Badger One, this is Coyote Six. How do you read? Over."

"This is Red Badger One. Load and clear, Coyote Six. Over," said Cox.

"Red Badger One, weapon up. 4 o'clock. Fire for effect on my signal," said Turner. "I want a nice spread around that office window. Over."

"Roger that, Coyote Six. Waiting for your go. Over," said Cox.

Turner gave the tarp a healthy yank pulling it off of Thunder. A hatch opened on the drone. The minigun rose and whipped around pointing toward the payroll office.

"Lowell, is that you?" said Turner to the empty window. "Come on, Staff Sergeant. Don't be a pussy."

Lowell's expression tightened. He had found someone deserving of his rage and nothing was going to stop him. He chambered a round into the submachine gun. "That's what he wants you to do, Lowell," said Billy watching his brother, hoping beyond hope that he'd listen to reason.

Lowell rose up from behind the desk and fired a burst from the submachine gun through the window.

Turner hit the deck and said, "Red Badger One, fire."

Lowell saw the barrels of the minigun start to spin and realized what was about to happen. He said, "Oh shit." He kicked over the steel desk in front of him and crouched behind it.

The six rotating barrels on Thunder's minigun sounded like a buzz-saw as they unleashed one hundred rounds per second. The noise was deafening and echoed off the concrete walls inside the building. Hundreds of hot empty shells clinked and formed a pile on the concrete floor in front of Turner's face. He rolled under the truck to avoid being burned by the hot brass.

The office walls were like paper, tattered to shreds by the hail of bullets.

Billy grabbed Tien and rolled on the floor until they were behind the payroll safe with Tien laying on top of Billy like lovers.

The steel desk that Lowell was hiding behind was shredded like Swiss cheese, starting at one end and moving toward Lowell. Lowell followed Billy's lead and jumped behind the safe, landing on Tien's back. Billy gasped for air from the extra weight. There wasn't much room, but laying on top of each other was the only way not to be killed by the barrage of bullets.

Thunder kept firing until the ceiling and walls of the office collapsed. "Red Badger One, ceasefire," said Turner into his radio headset.

The gunfire ceased and the weapon rotated to a stop. Smoke poured out of the ends of each barrel.

Turner rose from the floor and surveyed the damage. It was difficult to see through the dust cloud that had formed over the pile of debris. "Outstanding," said Turner to himself, impressed with Thunder's performance.

A corporal stepped from one of the vehicles and approached Turner. "Corporal, take your fire team and make sure whatever is under that rubble stays there, then join us at the site," said Turner.

"Roger that, Master Sergeant," said the corporal, motioning to the three MPs in the car.

The four MPs covered their mouths and noses with scarfs to keep the dust, almost assuredly filled with asbestos, from entering their lungs. They readied their weapons and moved toward the collapsed office.

Turner and the tow truck driver secured the tarp over Thunder and climbed back into the truck's cab.

"Everyone switch to secure radio comms," said Turner. "Let's move out."

The roll-up door at the front of the warehouse opened, and the convoy of trucks and cars rolled out on to the street.

Inside the warehouse, the four MPs approached the pile of rubble with caution as the dust settled. They used their rifle barrels to sift through the debris searching for a body. One of the MPs heard a hushed cough over by a mound of debris. He pushed broken ceiling panels aside to uncover Tien. The MP knelt and turned her over. She was covered in dust and wheezing like she couldn't breathe. "I got a live one over here. It's a woman," said the MP turning toward the corporal.

"No. Master Sergeant says they are all dead. Make it so," said the corporal.

The MP turned back and saw the pistol in Tien's hand pointed at his crouch. She fired two rounds to get his attention. She got it. He crumpled, dying as blood poured out of his wounds.

Lowell rose up from a pile of debris behind her and opened fire with the submachine gun killing one of the three remaining MPs. The other two MPs returned fire. Lowell dove for cover behind the safe. Billy pushed off a layer of debris, pulled the pin on the grenade he had taken off the lookout and tossed it. "Fire in the hole," yelled Billy.

The explosion killed the two MPs and kicked up more dust.

Lowell, Tien, and Billy coughed and spit, trying to clear their lungs. "That can't be good for ya," said Billy.

"We gotta move," said Lowell in between hacking and spitting. "We're gonna lose 'em."

They climbed to their feet, took the weapons and ammunition from the MPs and moved out of the building through the open roll-up door.

Outside the building, it was easier to breathe. The convoy was nowhere in sight. Tien pulled out her mobile, looked up a number and dialed. A NATO operator answered. "General Hanson's office," said Tien.

General Hanson was in conference with his staff when his secretary entered. "Sorry to interrupt, General. There's a Lieutenant Tien on the phone. She says it's urgent."

"Take a message," said Hanson.

"She said to tell you she found Thunder," said the secretary.

Hanson considered for a moment, then nodded to the secretary. She picked up the conference room phone, dialed an extension code to connect the call and handed the phone to Hanson. "This better not be bullshit, Lieutenant. You're in enough trouble as it is," said Hanson.

"It's not, General. I saw it with my own eyes. We found the drone," said Tien over the phone.

"So, where is it?"

"It just left a warehouse near the harbor in Antwerp."

"You lost it again?"

"For the moment, yes, sir. But it's on the back of a flatbed tow truck covered with a blue tarp. It's part of a convoy of civilian vehicles including two delivery trucks. We should be able to spot if from the air, but only if we hurry, General."

Hanson took a moment to think and said, "All right, Lieutenant. You've got yourself back in the ballgame. Don't fuck it up. You're on point until my deputy commander arrives. We'll send you combat air support, but it'll be coming in from Eindhoven. It'll take about an hour to get there."

"Thunder could be gone by then, General," said Tien.

"Then I suggest you find it, Lieutenant."

"Yes, sir."

"This number is good to contact you?"

"Yes, sir."

"Expect a call from staff. Good hunting, Lieutenant."

"Yes, sir. Thank you, sir."

"Don't thank me. Just find the damn thing," said Hanson and hung up.

Hanson turned to General Moretti, his deputy commander, "Make sure the Lieutenant gets what she needs. She's our best shot before this whole thing blows up in our faces."

"Yes, General," said Moretti.

Tien, Lowell, and Billy climbed into the rental car. "You gotta plan, L.T.?" said Lowell.

"We scour the harbor until we find them," said Tien.

"Maybe they're not here for the harbor," said Billy.

"What makes you think that?" said Tien.

"Why carry Thunder on the back of a flatbed tow truck?" said Billy. "It doesn't make sense. If they were gonna smuggle it aboard a ship, they would have it loaded in a cargo container or hidden in a shipment of pipes or something, like they did the weapons they sold to the Czech arms dealer, right? They could have kept it hidden by disguising it in the warehouse. But they didn't."

"Why do you suppose they didn't?" said Lowell.

"Because they don't care. They're not going to sell it. They're going to use it," said Billy.

"On what?" said Tien. "Turner is a thief, not a terrorist. What's his motivation?"

"Money. A lot I imagine," said Billy.

"You think he's gonna rob a bank?" said Lowell.

"No. Not a bank. He wouldn't need to come all this way if he just wanted to rob a bank. They've got plenty of banks in Germany," said Billy.

"What then?" said Tien.

"What's the one thing you can find in Antwerp, but nowhere else in the world?" said Billy.

EIGHTEEN

Antwerp's Diamond Quarter was located a short distance from the Central Train Station and measured about one square mile. The neighborhood was dominated by Jewish, Jain Indians, Armenians and Maronite Christian Lebanese traders known as diamantaires. Yiddish was the common language. Most of the area's restaurants were kosher and served a variety of ethnic dishes. Three hundred and eighty workshops served over three thousand brokers accommodated in the surrounding office buildings.

Eighty percent of the world's rough diamonds with a value in excess of fifty-four billion U.S. dollars passed through the four main diamond exchanges each year. Unknown to the outside world, all four of the exchanges housed their diamonds in the same centrally located storage facility below the street and connected by an underground network of tunnels used for safe transport of their diamonds when requested. The owners of the four exchanges subscribed to the concept of putting all of one's eggs in one basket… then watching that basket very closely. The common storage facility was a cost saving measure and allowed for substantial improvements in asset protection, including eight of the world's most secure vaults.

With the exception of a few very large stones, an uncut diamond was virtually untraceable. Lightweight and small in size, a fortune in diamonds could be carried in one's pocket without notice. For millennia diamonds have been the perfect currency for smugglers and those that would do evil.

The traders and tourists that crowded the promenade that divided the diamond quarter had no idea what was coming or that the world's largest diamond dump was just ten meters below their feet. It was just another autumn day in Antwerp. They ate their Belgian fries, snapped selfies and visited with one another on the benches and restaurant patios. Fortunately, traffic gave them a few more minutes of carefree chit-chat…

Antwerp's streets were narrow, like many cities in Europe. The cars were smaller than those in America and required less room. Just like in America there was always a delivery driver willing to clog a busy street by simply stopping in the middle of it to make a delivery. In this case, it was a cheese delivery van.

Cars quickly backed up and blocked Turner's convoy, pissing him off to no end. The honking and cursing in Dutch from the drivers didn't help lighten his mood. Turner was a man that lived by schedules and the cheese delivery van driver was messing up his timetable. "How far are we from the target?" said Turner.

"A little less than half a mile," said the tow truck driver.

"All right. Enough of this shit," said Turner, stepping from the truck cab.

"Where are you going, Master Sergeant?" said the tow truck driver.

"I'm gonna unclog this latrine," said Turner.

Turner radioed Cox, "Red Badger One, this is Coyote Six. Over."

"This is Red Badger One. Copy, Coyote Six," said Cox over the radio.

"Are you ready to rock-and-roll, Red Badger One?" said Turner.

"Absolutely, Coyote Six," said Cox over the radio.

"Standby, Red Badger One," said Turner.

Turner once again cut the ropes holding the tarp over Thunder. He stepped to the back of the tow truck. There was a Renault station wagon right behind the flatbed and it was blocked by a long line of cars and trucks. He motioned to the driver and said, "You. Out of the vehicle."

The driver flipped him off. "Have it your way," said Turner picking up the tow truck's flatbed control harness and pressing the ramp button.

The tow truck flatbed slid backward on heavy-duty rollers so it hovered over the front hood of the Renault. Turner pressed the tilt control and the front of the flatbed rose while the back lowered right onto the hood of the Renault, crushing it.

"Are you out of your fucking mind?" said the Renault driver stepping from his vehicle.

"Nope. But I got a schedule to keep," said Turner as he pulled out his pistol and shot the man in the forehead. He crumpled to the street dead. Drivers abandoned their cars and trucks and ran for their lives. The flatbed stopped in the middle of the Renault, unable to reach the street. "Red Badger One, that's as far as I can get ya. Over," said Turner.

"No problem, Coyote Six," said Cox.

Thunder's side panels slide upward revealing its wheels. Its legs extended raising the vehicle's chassis to give it high clearance. It drove off the back of the flatbed and over the Renault crushing it further. It crushed several other cars maneuvering to the sidewalk where it had some wiggle room.

"Red Badger One, see that Cheese truck?" said Turner.

"Affirmative, Coyote Six," said Cox.

"Make it Swiss, Red Badger One," said Turner.

"Roger that, Coyote Six," said Cox.

A panel opened and Thunder's cannon raised. It locked into position.

"Load HEAT," said Cox into his headset.

Thunder's autoloading system retrieved a HEAT round and loaded into main gun's breach. "HEAT up," said the drone's synthetic voice over the radio.

Cox checked the auto-targeting system and selected the cheese truck.

The drone rotated its wheels to horizontally align the barrel.

Cox squeezed the trigger on the joystick.

Thunder fired a HEAT round into the delivery van. The resulting explosion blew the van's sides, front and back outward like a balloon filled with too much helium. All of the windows in the surrounding vehicles and buildings shattered from the explosion's overpressure. "Away," said Thunder.

Only the van's drive train sat in a shallow crater in the street when the smoke cleared. "Outstanding," said Turner into his radio headset.

"Thunder, ceasefire main cannon," said Cox into his headset.

Thunder lowered the cannon and the panel closed.

The MP's and technicians in Turner's convoy jumped out of their vehicles and drove the abandoned cars out of their way. "This is Coyote six. It's taking too long. Everyone get back in their vehicles. Over," said Turner over the radio.

The team members returned to their vehicles and waited.

Inside the tow truck, Turner said to the driver, "Make me a path."

The tow truck drove forward like a snow plow crashing into cars and pushing them aside. The convoy moved up behind the tow truck slowly making progress through the traffic jam until it came to the remains of the delivery truck. The tow truck pushed the remains out of the way, and the convoy moved past the wreckage.

"You wanna load Thunder back up?" said the tow truck driver to Turner.
"Nah. We're close enough. It can hoof it on its own," said Turner.

Thunder followed behind the convoy. A Belgian police car with its lights flashing raced into the intersection behind Thunder and skidded to a stop.

The officers in the car jumped out and drew their sidearms. They hesitated, seeing the strange vehicle.

"Thunder, ready minigun," said Cox over the radio.

A panel opened and Thunder's minigun emerged. "Minigun up," said Thunder over the radio.

Cox targeted the police car with the control cockpit's joystick.

The minigun whipped around on its rotating mount and fired a one hundred round burst in less than a second. The officers and their vehicle were shredded.

"Thunder, ceasefire," said Cox over the radio.

The minigun disappeared into the drone and the panel closed.

Turner ordered a fire team of four MPs to take up a rearguard position behind Thunder as they traveled. Thunder was an integral part of the plan. The MPs weren't. Their job was security.

The convoy rolled across a cobblestone intersection and entered the diamond quarter. The buildings changed in appearance to opulent and of 18th Century design. Hundreds of jewelry stores displaying their finest pieces in their windows. The diamond exchanges were office buildings, almost non-descript as if reluctant to draw attention.

A security guard exited a jewelry store and drew his sidearm. He ordered a passing MP to put down his weapon. Another MP shot a three-round burst from his rifle into the guard's head. The guard collapsed dead.

Turner and his team moved on without giving the victim another thought. They all understood that once they had stolen Thunder and the first civilian was killed, there was little chance they would avoid capital punishment if their mission failed.

Approaching a promenade, Turner came to a line of stainless steel bollards running across the street to prevent vehicles from entering the promenade. "This is Coyote Six. Beaver team leader, bring up some detcord and take 'em out," said Turner over the radio. "Bulldog and Tiger Team elements take up defensive positions."

The MPs and technicians exited the vehicles and took up firing positions behind whatever cover they could find. The squad of engineers moved up and removed spools of detonation cord from their rucksacks. The black cables were filled with pentaerythritol tetranitrate – a high explosive.

Each engineer wrapped two lengths of detonation cord around the base of a bollard. Everyone cleared away as one of the engineers used a multi-port electronic detonator to ignite the separate cords. The cords exploded and the four steel bollards were instantly cut at their bases and toppled over. The engineers rolled the broken bollards out of the way. With the path clear, the convoy entered the promenade.

A Belgian police helicopter appeared overhead. A sniper in the aircraft's doorway took a shot at Thunder with a high-powered rifle. The bullet grazed off of Thunder's armor designed to deflect small arms fire.

An MP with a stinger missile launcher stepped from one of the vehicles and fired. The five-foot-long missile left the launch tube with a thump at an unimpressive rate of speed, until the missile reached a safe distance from the operator and the missile's propellant was ignited. The missile streaked into the sky leaving a trail of smoke and quickly reached Mach-Two. As it approached its target, the missile's guidance system switched from infrared to ultraviolet and retargeted from the aircraft's engine exhaust to the largest section of the fuselage – the passenger compartment. It struck the helicopter in the belly of the airframe. The helicopter burst into flames as it fell from the sky. Twisting out of control, it crashed into the front of a building and the wreckage plummeted to the ground killing all those inside plus two pedestrians.

"That should give 'em pause," said Turner, watching from the tow truck cab.

He was right of course. The Belgian police had had enough. Five officers killed in less than five minutes was the breaking point. The enemy they faced was military and it was up to their military to stop them. Not even their SWAT teams would be allowed to engage these criminals. Instead, the police were ordered to evacuate everyone still in the path of the rogue American soldiers.

The police moved the civilians still in the buildings out the back doors into the adjacent alleys away from the line of fire. Most of the guards watching over the jewelry stores and protecting the exchanges refused to leave. Many were ex-military and received good salaries that they did not want to give up if they failed to do their duty. They too were well-armed with submachine guns and wore body armor. They would make the Americans think twice about robbing the stores or exchanges they protected.

Turner saw this as an advantage. He was not afraid of the civilians or the guards, but he didn't want them to get in the way either. His team was still made up of young soldiers that would be prone to changing the level of their commitment to the mission if the blood-letting and body-count rose too high. Most of them had not fought in a war and did not fully understand the concept of collateral damage. He would pause the team for a moment and let the police do their work… but just for a moment. The more civilians out of their way the better.

Several blocks away, Tien, Billy, and Lowell watched the helicopter crash. "Where'd they get a stinger?" said Lowell.

"They were part of the weapons they stole from the armory," said Tien.

"Anything else we should be aware of?", said Billy.

"Only that they are well armed, well trained and will probably fight to the death since they know they will most likely be executed should their mission fail," said Tien.

"Good to know," said Billy.

Tien slowed the car to a stop as they came upon the wrecked police car. "Jesus," said Tien seeing the shredded bodies of the police officers.

"If anyone ever wanted to know what war looks like, that there wouldn't be too far off," said Lowell.

"I've seen death, but this…" said Tien.

"Poor bastards," said Billy. "They should have been warned."

"We did warn them. They didn't listen," said Tien. "Civilians just don't understand what modern weapons can do."

"Thunder didn't do this on its own. Somebody pulled the trigger," said Lowell.

Billy looked at the trail of wreckage the convoy had left and said, "Well, at least they left us a trail."

"We should approach on foot," said Lowell. "If we all roll up in this thing, they'll just do the same to us as they did to them. On foot, we can use the buildings for cover."

"I agree," said Tien.

They exited the car. Tien opened the trunk and pulled out the cases for the Javelin. She opened the case and began assembling it. "You ever use one of those before?" said Lowell.

"I read the manual," said Tien.

"You know it weighs fifty pounds," said Lowell.

"I am aware of its weight, Staff Sergeant. Like I said… I read the manual."

"It can be a little nose-heavy and throw your aim off," said Lowell. "Plus they'll probably be shooting at ya. That's always a challenge when you're trying to focus on the target. That's something they don't mention in the manual."

"Good to know," said Tien. "I'll keep it in mind."

"Are you gonna use the top-attack flight profile or the direct attack mode?" said Lowell.

"I haven't decided," said Tien. "What would you suggest?"

"I would suggest you let me handle it, so we don't get our asses shot off," said Lowell.

"All right," said Tien. "But only on my command."

"Yes, Ma'am," said Lowell. "Assuming you're still alive to give the command."

"Very funny, Staff Sergeant," said Tien.

"Wasn't meant to be, Ma'am," said Lowell.

Lowell took the different pieces of the Javelin weapon system and assembled it like the seasoned warrior he was. "Weapon's ready, L.T.," said Lowell hoisting the weapon on his shoulder.

"It's Lieutenant, not L.T., Staff Sergeant," said Tien.

"Lieutenant it is, Ma'am. But it don't really matter much. We're all gonna be dead in about five minutes anyway," said Lowell moving off down the street.

Billy and Tien followed. They stayed close to the buildings and used doorways as temporary cover as they moved forward through the carnage of wrecked vehicles and passed bodies of civilians lying in the street. Anyone that had mounted any level of resistance had been killed without hesitation. "How can they just kill like that? Without remorse?" said Tien.

"They're human. We want something bad enough, we can justify almost anything," said Lowell. "Right, Billy?"

Billy didn't respond to Lowell's cutting question, but the reference was not lost on him. He had killed in the name of justice, or at least that is what he told himself. He knew Lowell had too, but he chose not to provoke a fight. They had their hands full. Now was not the time.

Turner took the temporary halt to recheck his map and the path they would take to the target. The entry point to the underground vaults was located in the center of the diamond quarter. It was less than a 10-minute walk and he was anxious to get there. "This is Coyote Six. Alright men, let's get to it," said Turner to his men. "Bulldog team on foot providing security. Tiger and Beaver teams in the vehicles. Out."

Billy, Lowell, and Tien approached the intersection. They could see Thunder in the distance at the rear of the convoy. They crouched down behind an abandoned car. "Okay, what's the plan, Lieutenant?" said Lowell.

"We sneak up on them and destroy Thunder with the Javelin," said Tien.

"You do realize it cost almost a quarter of a billion dollars to develop that prototype?" said Lowell.

"We don't have much choice. They've already killed multiple civilians and police officers. If we don't stop Thunder they're just gonna go right on killing. So I say we destroy it before it can do any more damage," said Tien.

"Okay. And what do we do when they realize what we have done and open fire with everything else they stole?" said Lowell.

"I think running is a pretty good strategy in that case," said Tien.

"You're not gonna get any argument from me," said Billy.

"We're just gonna let Turner go?" said Lowell.

"No. We're gonna let NATO capture Turner and his men," said Tien. "Taking Thunder out is our highest priority. After that, this thing becomes just another criminal investigation. We follow procedure and procedure dictates that unless human life is at stake we wait for backup."

"Seems like the pussy way out, if you pardon my French, Ma'am," said Lowell.

"You got a better plan, Staff Sergeant?" said Tien, losing her patience.

"Yeah. We kill 'em," said Lowell.

"All of them?" said Tien. "With a couple of submachine guns and pistols? Last time I looked we were outgunned and outnumbered."

"She's got a point, Lowell," said Billy. "'Sides, it ain't like he's gonna get away. We can follow him and his men and call in their location to the NATO forces when they arrive."

"You don't know Turner," said Lowell. "He's thought through every detail of this thing and he's prepared for any eventuality. We don't kill him now while we've got 'im in our sights, we could lose him for good. We could time our shots. Kill Turner and Thunder at the same time."

"No, Staff Sergeant. We are not just going to assassinate him," said Tien.

"Because he's such a nice guy?"

"No. Because the U.S. Army abides by the law. He and his men may be murderers, but they have a right to trial," said Tien. "End of discussion. You have your orders, Staff Sergeant Gamble. Now take out Thunder or turn your weapon back over to me and I'll do it."

"All right, Ma'am," said Lowell. "You're the officer. I'll do it."

"What's the best angle of attack? In the rear like most tanks?" said Tien.

"No. With Thunder, it don't matter. The armor is the same all the way around. I just need to get close enough to make sure I don't miss," said Lowell. "I say we split up. Billy and you are one fire team and I am the other. We move down the opposite sides of the street, then cross out of their line of sight. We use the buildings for cover like we've been doing. If we're discovered, it'll be up to Billy and you to draw their attention away from me. You don't need to be heroes. Just fire a few rounds, then take cover until I fire. Then we skedaddle back to this point and trail them at a distance until backup arrives. That okay with you, Lieutenant?"

"Yes. It sounds like a good plan, Staff Sergeant," said Tien. "We should get going before they get too far ahead of us. Good luck."

Tien and Billy moved down one side of the intersecting street and Lowell moved in the opposite direction down the other side of the street.

Once they were out of Turner's sight line, they crossed over and moved back to the corners of the buildings on opposite sides of the street. Tien gave Lowell a nod and they moved forward toward Thunder and the convoy, staying close to the buildings, ducking in and out of doorways.

The convoy resumed its journey toward the vaults. The rearguard took up hidden positions in the building doorways and kept watch. They didn't expect much resistance after Thunder's show of force. Since going rogue, the discipline in the team was growing lax. Their fear of Turner's boot up their asses and the big payout were the only things keeping them in line. They visited we each other talking about what they would do with their share.

Lowell moved up closer as Thunder moved away. He knew Thunder would soon be out of range. The Javelin weapon system's thermal sight used a Focal Plane Array to capture and track the target. It required thirty-seconds of cooling before it could be used effectively. Lowell powered up the system to begin the cooling process.

One of the MPs caught a glimpse of Lowell as he ducked into a doorway. The MP moved to investigate. As he moved up, he saw Lowell and the Javelin he was carrying. He raised his rifle and took aim at Lowell's head.

Billy spotted the MP getting ready to fire at Lowell. He raised his pistol and fired.

The bullet hit the MP on the right side of his body armor and knocked the wind out of him. He collapsed to the walkway. The other MPs moved up behind the fallen MP and fired at Billy and Tien.

Turner heard the gunshots and called his men, "Bulldog, this is Coyote Six. What the hell is going on? Over."

"This is Bulldog Three. It's Staff Sergeant Gamble and two others," said the MP gasping for breath. "He's got a portable launch tube. Probably a Javelin."

"Shit," said Turner. "Bulldog, kill him, damn it."
"Wilco, Six," said the MP.
"Red Badger One, this is Coyote Six. You copy?" said Turner into his headset.
"This is Red Badger One. I am on it, Coyote Six," said Cox over the radio. "Activating counter-measures system. Over."

While Billy and Tien exchanged fire with the MPs, Lowell looked down at the Javelin's readout. It turned green signaling it was ready. Lowell raised the weapon and took aim through the infrared sight. He centered the crosshairs on the middle of the back of Thunder's fuselage as it moved away. It was not the best angle, but he was running out of time and decided to take the shot. He squeezed the trigger and the weapon fired.

The missile left the launch tube with a dull thump and its guidance fins snapped open. It traveled ten feet from the launch tube before the main motor ignited and propelled the missile toward its target.

Thunder's automated counter-measures system correctly identified the threat as it approached and took control of the drone. A panel on the top of the drone opened and a canister launcher popped up. It fired five flares and chaff canisters into the air above the drone and four smoke grenades around the vehicle. The chaff canisters exploded into metallic streamers, while the flares created starbursts of burning magnesium. The result was a dome of confusion making it impossible for the infrared missile to identify the drone's outline and heat signatures. Thunder also took an evasive maneuver to further mask its whereabouts beneath the dome of smoke. Its four wheels turned in unison and the vehicle crabbed to one side then crouched down to create a low profile. Losing its target in the chaos, the missile flew to Thunder's last position and passed less than a foot from the drone without hitting it. The missile slammed into a building and exploded sending flames and glass into the street.

"Fuck," said Lowell seeing that his shot had failed. He dropped the empty launch tube and pulled back from his position in the doorway. He whistled to Billy and Tien and motioned for them to pull back too.

The rearguard MPs held their position but kept up their fire as Billy, Tien, and Lowell retreated. "Coyote Six, this is Bulldog Three. Staff Sergeant Gamble and his team have retreated. Should we pursue? Over," said an MP over the radio.

"You're damn right you should pursue, Bulldog. I want Sergeant Gamble's head and your mission ain't over until I have it. This is what you're getting paid for, so don't fuck it up. Six, out."

The rear guard MPs moved back down the promenade in the direction Lowell was headed. They spread out. They were in hunt mode.

Lowell rendezvoused with Billy and Tien at the place they had discussed. "I don't want to hear any shit from you, Billy," said Lowell.

"It ain't your fault, Lowell," said Billy.

"I said shut up," said Lowell.

"If you two are through... I've used up most of my ammunition," said Tien.

"Me too. I've only got three rounds in my last clip," said Billy. "If we get in another firefight, we're gonna be in a world of hurt."

"I'll get us some," said Lowell.

"From where?" said Tien.

"From our enemy," said Lowell.

"You and the Lieutenant should follow Thunder and Turner. I'll get us the ammunition," said Billy.

"The hell you say," said Lowell.

"Lowell, it makes sense. Hunting down Thunder is a military operation. Getting ammunition is an errand," said Billy.

"An errand?" said Tien.

"Well... a dangerous errand, but yeah," said Billy. "I can do it. You know I'm sneaky, Lowell."

"Yeah, you're sneaky all right," said Lowell.

"Then it's settled. Billy, you go after the ammunition. Staff Sergeant Gamble, you're with me. We'll sidestep the MPs and go after Thunder. Where should we rendezvous?"

"I don't think we're gonna have any trouble finding each other. Just follow the path of death and destruction," said Billy.

"All right. Let's get going," said Tien.

Billy handed Lowell his pistol. "What's this?" said Lowell.

"I ain't gonna need it. This is close up work," said Billy. "I'll catch up as soon as I have some ammo."

"Billy?"

"Yeah, Lowell."

"Don't fuck up and get yourself killed. We need that ammo."

"No fucking up. Got it, Lowell. Really useful advice."

"Don't be a smartass," said Lowell. "You know what I mean."

"Yeah... I guess I do," said Billy.

Lowell took the pistol from Billy and they moved off. Billy in one direction, Lowell and Tien in another.

Billy moved through several abandoned cars using them to hide his movements, including an old Volkswagen Beetle. From his vantage point, he saw the MPs spreading out as they approached the intersection. He reached up and snapped off the Beetle's old-style antenna at his base. He moved to a doorway and extended the antenna as far as it would go. He waited until the first MP moved past the doorway. Billy whipped the MP in the face with the antenna. He grabbed the stunned MP by the vest and swung him around into the doorway. Billy punched the MP in the face three times, breaking his nose and knocking him unconscious. Billy grabbed the MP and held him up as another MP, hearing the scuffle, rounded the corner into the doorway. Billy pulled the unconscious MPs' sidearm and fired twice into the second MP hitting him just above his armored vest. The second MP crumpled to the ground, dead. Billy pulled off their web belts and vests holding their extra ammunition.

He picked up their weapons and started to move off when a burst of machinegun fire drove him back into the doorway. The two other MPs were moving up fast on his position, firing as they approached. The two MPs spread out giving them two different angles of attack. Billy prepared to return fire. He laid down the submachine guns and pulled out the two pistols. He figured he could dive into the street once the first MP was close enough. He was pretty sure he could kill him if he timed it right. The second MP was the problem. There was nothing Billy could do about him, but hope he was a lousy shot.

The first MP approached, Billy leaped out of the doorway and fired both pistols several times. As he had hoped, his aim was true and one of the bullets entered the MPs' forehead. He fell dead. Billy landed on the ground. He looked for the second MP and saw him leveling his submachine gun to fire at point-blank range. A burst of fire sailed over Billy's head from behind and killed the second MP before he could fire. It was Lowell. Tien was beside him. Billy smiled and said, "Nice shot."

"I told ya not to fuck up, Billy," said Lowell.

"Yeah, ya did, Lowell," said Billy with a smile, never happier to see his big brother.

"You're lucky we decided to go this way."

"Yeah. I am," said Billy. "I got the ammo and more guns than I think we need."

"You can never have too many guns," said Lowell.

"I suppose not," said Billy.

"If you two are done with your family reunion, I think we should keep moving," said Tien.

"Roger that, Lieutenant," said Lowell.

They gathered the weapons and ammunition. The MP that Billy whipped and punched in the face groaned as he began to come around. Lowell waited until the Lieutenant looked the other way, then kicked him in the head, knocking him unconscious again. They moved off down the promenade in the direction of the convoy.

The convoy approached a square with a large building in the center and a narrow vehicle ramp to one side.

The MPs spread out, taking up firing positions around the square. Thunder moved toward the entrance to the ramp. The single-lane ramp led down below the street to a highly secured loading dock that was used for shipments of diamonds flown in from around the world. An abandoned armored truck was parked in front of the dock. "Shit," said Turner upon seeing the armored truck. "If it ain't one thing, it's another."

Turner sent a team of MPs down to check the armored truck, hoping they might be able to drive it out of the ramp. No luck. "Coyote Six, this is Bulldog Niner. It's locked up tighter than a frog's ass," said the MP over the radio.

Guards inside the high-security loading dock opened fire through gun portals and killed the MP. "God damn it," said Turner.

"Beaver Team, this is Coyote Six. Bring up two satchel charges and smoke. Breach that loading dock. Over," said Turner.

"This is Beaver Six. Wilco, Coyote Six," said the lead engineer.

The four engineers moved down the ramp and split into two to approach from both sides using the armored vehicle as cover. One of the engineers on the left side of the armored truck threw a smoke grenade up onto the loading dock. The loading dock filled with smoke making it impossible for the guards inside to see what was going on outside the loading dock. They fired wildly through their gun portals. The two engineers on the left side of the armored truck opened fire, spraying the loading dock with bullets. It had no effect against the concrete wall and steel door, but it did divert the guards' attention. The two engineers from the right side of the armored truck pulled the rings on the mechanical fuses of each of their satchel charges. They ran forward and threw the backpacks in front of the steel door. The engineers retreated, running back up the ramp and leaping over the concrete side walls at the top. The charge exploded and the ground shook. A ball of flame rolled up and out the ramp. The armored truck rocked from the explosion, but did not move.

Turner watched as the smoke cleared. The loading dock was still blocked by the abandoned armored truck, but the loading dock door and most of the concrete wall was breached. The guards inside had been blown to pieces from the explosion. Turner radioed the tow truck driver, "Heavy Lift One, this is Coyote Six. Pull that piece of shit out of our way. Over."

"This is Heavy Lift One. Wilco, Coyote Six," said the tow truck driver.

The tow truck backed down the ramp and the driver jumped out of the cab. He pulled the cable from the winch and attached it to the front axle of the armored truck. He operated the winch from its control harness. The winch strained to pull the armored truck. It didn't move. "Coyote Six, this is Heavy Lift One. It's too heavy for the winch," said the driver over his radio headset.

"This is Coyote Six. Well, we'll just have to lighten the load of that son of a bitch," said Turner. "Move out of the way, Heavy Lift One."

"Red Badger One, this is Coyote Six. Get your ass down here and fire on that armored truck. Over," said Turner over the radio.

"This is Red Badger One. Wilco, Coyote Six. Over," said Cox over the radio.

The tow truck driver unhitched the cable, climbed back into the truck's cab and drove the tow truck off the ramp.

Thunder pulled to a stop at the top of the ramp. "Red Badger One, this is Coyote Six. Give me some HEAT, son," said Turner over the radio.

"Thunder, load HEAT," said Cox over his headset.

The auto-loader inside Thunder retrieved a HEAT shell and pushed it into the main gun's breach. "HEAT up," said the drone's synthetic voice over the radio.

Cox targeted the armored truck and squeezed the trigger on the joystick.

The high-velocity HEAT round crashed through the armored truck's front window and hit the front wall of the armored compartment. The shaped charge inside the shell exploded punching a small hole in the armor and creating a molten jet stream of liquid metal. The liquid metal jet penetrated the armored compartment and spread out like thousands of high-velocity needles. One of the white-hot needles pierced the gas tank and ignited the fuel blowing the vehicle apart from the inside. The armored truck leaped into the air and the remains crashed down on its side.

Debris was scattered across the ramp and loading dock. "Away," said Thunder's synthetic voice over the radio.

Cox moved Thunder out of the way and the tow truck backed down the ramp. The driver climbed out of the cab and used the truck's fire extinguisher to put out the fires on the debris and on what remained of the truck's drivetrain still blocking the ramp. Engineers put gloves on and picked up the pieces of smoking debris on the ramp to clear a path. The driver wrapped the cable around the axle and used the winch to pull the smoking hulk of metal onto the tow truck's flatbed. He drove off the ramp leaving a clear path to the loading dock.

Billy, Tien, and Lowell heard the explosions as they approached the square. They crouched down behind a car and watched from a distance. "What the hell are they doing?" said Lowell.

"I have no idea," said Billy, watching. "Looks like they're breaking into a parking garage."

"Why would they pass up all these jewelry stores only to break into a parking garage?" said Tien. "It doesn't make any sense."

"They won't need Thunder to break into a jewelry store. They've got enough firepower to keep a small army at bay. Why steal Thunder?"

"Obviously they are up to something," said Billy. "This location is in the center of the diamond quarter."

"So?" said Lowell.

"I'm just making an observation. You know… thinking out loud," said Billy.

"Well… You're supposed to be the smart one. Think better," said Lowell.

"And faster," said Tien.

Thunder moved back down the ramp and approached the loading dock. Thunder's minigun raised from out of its hidden compartment. Its targeting system scanned the hallway inside the loading dock. There were no targets available.

Two engineers approached the breached loading dock and used portable circular saws with diamond blades to cut away excess concrete and rebar still blocking the entrance to the vaults. The other two engineers kept watch on the hallway inside the facility.

Although Turner did not believe that anyone inside the facility could launch a credible attack against Thunder, he still was not taking any chances. "Bulldog Two, this is Coyote Six. Send a fire team up that tunnel and make sure we've got clear egress. Over," said Turner over the radio.

"This is Bulldog Two. On our way, Six," said the team leader.

Four MPs moved into the facility and up the tunnel with their weapons at the ready. They found no resistance. "Coyote Six, this is Bulldog Two. Tunnel is clear. Over," said the team leader.

"Bulldog Two, take up firing positions and wait for us there. We're coming in. Coyote Six, out."

The facility was abandoned. Any guards inside that had seen their fellow guards slaughtered by the satchel charges had decided that they were not being paid enough to risk their lives against such a formidable enemy. Besides, the diamonds were safe.

The vaults were impenetrable when they were locked down, and they had been when word first came of a possible threat. They would wait out the intruders and let the military deal with them.

Turner's engineers with the portable saws finished their cutting and used crowbars to move the concrete debris out of the path into the interior.

Thunder locked its back wheels and rose up like a dog begging for food. Placing its front wheels on the higher part of the loading dock, it climbed up like a mechanical monster, keeping its minigun trained on the hallway. The targeting system had identified the MPs inside as friendly and would not fire upon them even if a firefight broke out. Thunder retracted its wheels until they were no wider than the outer armor. It fit in the hallway with one foot to spare on each side. Its ability to crab its wheels would allow it to move around the tight corners within the facility. It was like it was perfectly designed for this particular mission.

The technicians and engineers unloaded the vehicles and carried the crates of equipment, explosives, weapons and ammunition inside the underground facility, using heavy-duty dollies to help with the heavy loads.

Billy, Lowell, and Tien watched from a distance. Tien's phone rang and she answered it. She listened for a minute, then hung up. "Calvary's almost here," she said.

"I think they're too late," said Billy.

"Why's that?" said Tien.

"Looks like they're going to ground," said Billy. "There'll be hell to pay if they dig in."

"It don't make sense," said Lowell. "Thunder can't maneuver underground. They're putting their best player on the bench."

"We can't see a damn thing from back here. We've got to get closer," said Billy.

"All right," said Tien.

"If they see us and bring Thunder into play, we won't stand a chance," said Lowell.

"Ain't like you to run scared, Lowell," said Billy.

"I ain't scared, Billy," said Lowell. "I just know what Thunder can do in the hands of a trained killer like Turner. We can't stop 'em if we're dead."

"I think we can get closer without being seen if we use the buildings as cover. We can go around and use the back alleys for our approach," said Billy.

"We'll lose sight of 'em if we do that," said Lowell.

"Okay. I'll stay here. I can keep watch and wait for the NATO troops to arrive. You two go have a closer look," said Tien.

"Affirmative, Lieutenant," said Lowell.

Billy and Lowell moved off, going back the way they came to use the alleys for cover. Tien continued to watch.

Each member of Turner's team put on a gas mask before entering the facility. Turner was sure there would be some sort of defensive system that would use knock-out gas to protect the facility from intruders. He was right, but the automated defense system control box was located within the loading dock and had been damaged in the explosion. It was useless.

The team members followed Thunder as it rolled into the hallway. The MPs outside kept watch until the last technician and engineer was inside, then they too collapsed down the ramp, through the breach and into the facility. No MPs from the team were left outside to keep watch for approaching threats. They had trapped themselves inside... just as they planned like a dead Pharaoh has himself buried deep in a pyramid surrounded by his treasure.

NINETEEN

Thunder rolled down the tunnel, its auto-targeting system identifying and analyzing anything that moved to determine if it was a threat. The MPs leapfrogged, keeping each other covered as they advanced, checking every doorway for hidden occupants. They found none.

Once the team reached the end of the first tunnel, the technicians opened one of the weapon crates they have brought with them. They pulled out a beefy tripod and a ROW – remote-controlled heavy machine gun. Originally designed to destroy armored personnel carriers and light tanks, the ROW's .50 caliber ammunition was capable of piercing 6 inches of steel plate. The remote-controlled weapon system was mounted on the tripod and pointed back down the tunnel the way they have come. The engineers set up sandbags filled with lead shot to form a protective wall in front of the ROW. The ROW had been modified with a radio transmitter that allowed Specialist Cox to operate the weapon from the remote control station he had set up in the penthouse. Anyone or anything entering the tunnel from outside the facility would be in the sights of the ROW auto-targeting system. The ROWs auto-targeting system was fast and could even identify, target and destroy a missile if given enough warning.

In addition to the tunnel leading to the loading dock, the facility had two more tunnels leading from the vaults to the basements of the four exchanges. By keeping all diamond transfers underground, the exchange owners had virtually eliminated the risk of a robbery and drastically reduced the cost of guards and armored vehicles formerly used for transport.

Turner and his team set up two more ROWs, one for each of the exchange tunnels. There was no other way in or out of the facility.

From his control station in the hotel penthouse, Specialist Cox could monitor each of the three tunnels and fire the appropriate ROW if a breach was attempted.

It was never the plan of the owners of the vaults to defend any intrusion into the facility beyond the highly trained guards that had already been killed. Instead, the vault doors would automatically close at the first sign of a robbery. They could only be reopened with codes the personnel inside the facility did not process. Hostages were of little use since they could not unlock the vaults. The facility would be evacuated of all personnel and the situation monitored on the three hundred security cameras - some hidden some not - spread throughout the facility. Antwerp's SWAT officers had yearly training exercises for such a breach and were familiar with every square foot of the facility. It was only a matter of time until they retook the facility and apprehended the intruders. It was a well-thought-out plan for anyone that was foolish enough to break into the world's most secure civilian facility... almost anyone.

A Belgian Air Force A109 helicopter swept in over the square and hovered, searching for a target. It found nothing. The Italian-made helicopter was armed with a remote-controlled .50-cal machine gun under its fuselage and twin rocket pods on its stubby wings.

Three Belgian Army VBMR Griffon armored personnel carriers rolled into the square and pulled to a stop. Each Griffon had a remote gun turret with a 7.65mm machine gun and a 40mm grenade autolauncher. The gunner inside each Griffon scanned the area for threats. Seeing none, each Griffon opened its back door and eight soldiers climbed out and took up defensive positions outside the vehicle using cars and concrete walls for protection. Troop trucks rolled in behind the Griffons and seventy more soldiers dismounted and took up defensive positions.

Tien kept low and moved behind the parked vehicles in the square as she made her way over to the Griffons. Two soldiers swung their rifles around as Tien approached. Tien stopped, set down her weapon and raised her hands to show she was not a threat. "Lieutenant Tien U.S. Army. I need to speak with your commander," she said.

One of the soldiers picked up her weapon and motioned for her to follow him. They approached Captain Peeters, the company commander. The soldier spoke to him in Dutch and motioned to Tien.

"You are Lieutenant Tien?" said Peeters.

"Yes, sir," said Tien saluting.

"My men don't salute while in the field, Lieutenant. It makes the officers a target," said Peeters.

"Of course, sir," said Tien slightly embarrassed. She should have known that, she thought.

"Can you brief me on the situation?" said Peeters.

"Yes, sir. My team and I have been tracking the suspects for the past week. I counted twenty-three, but there could be more we don't know about. They are commanded by a Master Sergeant Turner," said Tien.

"They stole some kind of tank?" said Peeters.

"It's not a tank. It's an anti-tank drone. It had just completed its final field tests when it was hijacked," said Tien.

"A drone?" said Peeters, incredulous.

"It would be a mistake to underestimate it, sir. It's a mean little son of a bitch. I've seen what it can do and you don't want to mess with it if you can avoid it."

"So, where is it?"

"Ten minutes ago it went underground along with all the members of Turner's team. Down that ramp over there," said Tien, motioning.

"*Kut!*" said Peeters seeing the ramp.

"I assume that's not good?"

"No. It's not good."

"What's down that ramp?"

Peeters considered for a moment and said, "The vaults for the diamond exchanges."

"Vaults. How much are we talking about?"

"Dollars or Euros?"

"Does it matter?"

"No. It's in the billions either way."

"Shit!"

"Yes. Shit is correct," said Peeters. "That drone of yours, what is its armament?"

"It can fire a sabot if that's what you're getting at," said Tien.

"Yes. That's what I was getting at," said Peeters, disheartened. "What kind of armor does it have?"

"Well, that's the good news. Light armor. If you can catch it above ground, I'm pretty sure your helicopter's rocket pod could take it out of commission if not destroy it completely. Do you have any shoulder-mounted anti-tank launchers?"

"Yes. In each of the Griffons."

"I would get them deployed ASAP. They should be able to penetrate its armor. But make your men are aware that it has reactive camouflage and an auto-defensive system that's very effective. We've already taken one shot at it with a Javelin and missed."

"All right. I will see that they are deployed right away."

"The ammunition for your machine guns, armor-piercing or full-metal jacket?"

"Full-metal jacket, unfortunately. We were at the firing range when the call came in and didn't have time to stop at the armory. Will it penetrate?"

"I don't know. The drone's armor is lightweight, but it's made of a new type of composite metal."

"I guess we'll find out the hard way," said Peeters.

"Two members of my team are doing reconnaissance in those buildings on the right side of the square," said Tien pointing. "I would hate to have them mistaken for the enemy."

"I'll inform my men and the air force. Keep me advised if they find anything," said Peeters.

"Absolutely, Captain Peeters," said Tien, moving off.

Billy and Lowell moved through an alley. "I think the other side of this building is the closest to the ramp," said Billy pointing.

Lowell tried to open the back door. It was locked. "It's locked tighter than a tick on a dog," said Lowell.

"Should we knock?" said Billy.

"Screw that. We're in a hurry," said Lowell as he raised his boot to kick the door in.

"Wait," said Billy. "Let me. You don't wanna pop another staple."

"You saying I can't do it?"

"No, Lowell. I know you can do. But be smart for a change. There's a lot at stake here and I don't need to be playing nursemaid if you bust yourself open, just cuz you're a stubborn jackass," said Billy raising his boot and kicking the door in. It took three tries.

"I could've done in one," said Lowell pushing past Billy and entering the building.

Billy and Lowell moved cautiously through the hallway and into the building's reception area. The interior was spacious and opulent. "What the hell is this place?" said Lowell. "Looks like a New Orleans whorehouse."

"It's a diamond exchange. Like a wholesaler for jewelers and diamond cutters."

"How the hell you know that?"

"Googled it."

"So, where are all the guards?"

"Don't know. I doubt they do any swapping down in the lobby. Probably moved upstairs to protect the diamonds when they heard the explosions and gunshots."

"Pussies," said Lowell.

They moved toward the front windows and stooped down behind a heavy wooden desk as they looked out. They saw the helicopter, the Griffons and the other vehicles. They saw the soldiers in their firing positions. "Looks like the cavalry arrived," said Billy.

"Poor bastards have no idea what they're facing," said Lowell.

"We still can't see shit," said Billy. "We've got to get inside and see what they are up to."

"You go right ahead and march down that ramp. My guess is Turner has his men waiting in ambush for anyone that tries to follow them."

Lowell called Tien and reported that they had arrived. She told him the ramp led to the diamond vaults. He hung up. "Well, I'm pretty sure I know what they're up to," said Lowell.

"What's that?"

"L.T. says there are diamond vaults below the street. The exchanges use them to store their diamonds."

"Can Thunder penetrate a vault?"

"Probably. Don't imagine it would be much tougher than a main battle tank with composite armor," said Lowell as he considered. "Thing is... the sabot shell they'd use only makes a hole the size of a silver dollar. Don't know how they'd get the diamonds out through a hole that small."

"I have no idea, but I am betting they do. This whole thing seems well planned out," said Billy.

"It's the military. We plan everything possible, then prepare for the impossible," said Lowell.

"If they're successful, how are they going to escape?" said Billy

"How in the hell am I supposed to know?" said Lowell.

"You know Turner better than anyone here. You fought by his side. What will he do?" said Billy. "Come on, Lowell. Use your noggin for once."

Lowell considered and said, "Turner knows what he and his men will be facing. Even with all their armament, they won't stand a chance by themselves. He'll send Thunder out first and have it clear a path before he attempts an escape."

"Will it succeed?"

"If I was operating it... maybe. But Specialist Cox is a wonk, not a warrior. Any action he's seen has been simulated. The real world is more unpredictable."

"You think he'll make a mistake?"

"Technically, no. He's a better operator than I am when it comes to controlling Thunder. But strategically... maybe..."

"So, once Thunder attacks, then what?"

"Turner and his men will stay hidden until most of the threats have been destroyed. They'll come out and secure the area."

"They won't just make a run for it?"

"No. Turner won't leave himself open for a rear attack. They'll secure the area before making their move. My guess is that they'll go on foot at least in the beginning. Any vehicle would be exposed to aerial attack. On foot, they can use buildings for cover. They'll use Thunder as a rearguard and hope the NATO forces focus on attacking Thunder, rather than Turner and his men. They'll probably split up at some point and try to mix in with the civilians. Rendezvous at a predetermined point once they are out of danger."

"So, that's his plan?"

"I didn't say that."

"What do you mean?"

"That's what I think he will do. But Turner knows that. He's too smart and too experienced to be predictable."

"Well… I guess we don't know what we don't know."

"That's the stupidest thing I have ever heard you say, Billy. You sound like a fucking fortune cookie."

Billy chuckled and said, "Yeah, I kinda do, don't I?"

Once Turner's team had cleared the facility and set up their defenses, they moved into a cavernous space – the vault chamber. The chamber was built like a rotunda with the eight exchange vaults laid out in a semi-circle. The vault doors were impressive and gave the impression of invincibility. Turner looked at the vaults and smiled.

The engineers moved to one of the walls at the end of the chamber. They used laser tape-measures to identify a spot on the wall and marked it with a green felt tip pen. They measured out from the mark and placed a series of explosive charges about the size and shape of a small garage door. Everyone in the chamber placed a set of hearing protector headsets over their ears to dampen the sound. They sought cover down the tunnels away from the blast radius. Turner made a call on his mobile phone. De Jong answered. "Clear," said Turner and hung up.

The engineers used an electronic detonator to set off the explosives. The explosion was powerful and rocked the facility. After a few minutes, the dust and smoke cleared to reveal that most of the concrete had been blown to bits, but layers of steel rebar crisscrossed the opening.

Through the lattice of rebar, Turner saw Meijer and De Jong standing in the basement of the building next door. They had already cut away the concrete and rebar on their side of the wall between the two buildings. "Outstanding," said Turner.

The men on both sides of the wall used their portable circular saws to cut through the rebar and create a shallow tunnel between the two buildings.

The four engineers removed eight fire hoses from one of the cases they had brought with them. They entered the office building basement through the tunnel and walked over to the exposed water main pipe on the opposite side of the basement. They attached the eight fire hoses to eight portable gas-powered pumps stationed next to the water main's access chamber and attached to the Storz couplers. They unraveled the fire hoses and stored the remaining hose rolls next to the tunnel entrance on the office building side where they would be spared any damage from explosions inside the vault facility.

The engineers moved back through the tunnel into the vault chamber.

Corporal Wright pulled out a portable computer tablet from his rucksack. He downloaded the schematic that Visser had purchased and Cox had been studying. He opened the file. The schematic of the vault door appeared on the tablet's screen. A cross-mark showed the exact location of the entry point into the vault. Wright used a laser tape-measure to find the exact position on the vault door and marked it with a green felt tip pen.

Wright repeated the same process for all eight vault doors, marking them each with his green felt-tip pen. When he'd finished the last one, he motioned to Turner that everything was ready.

Thunder entered the chamber from the hallway and moved into position in front of the first vault door but back away as far as possible from the door to prevent damage from the explosions.

Inside the hotel's penthouse, Cox maneuvered Thunder's targeting system using the control console. He lined up the system's cross-hairs on the green cross-mark Corporal Wright had made. The system flashed a warning that the acquired target was too close for safe detonation. Cox entered an override command and the warning changed to indicate that the system was ready. "Coyote Six, Red Badger One is ready. Over," said Cox into the radio headset.

Back inside the vault chamber, Turner responded in his headset, "This is Coyote Six. Copy that, Red Badger One. Standby." Turner ordered everyone out of the chamber. They moved around the corners and down the hallways. They each put on their hearing protector headsets. "Red Badger One, this is Coyote Six. You are clear to engage. Out," said Turner.

"Thunder, load sabot," said Cox into his headset.

Inside Thunder, the autoloader pulled a sabot shell from its protective tube and loaded it into the main gun's breach. The breach slide closed. "Sabot up," said Thunder over the radio.

Cox rechecked the placement of the crosshairs. "Fire in the hole," said Cox over the radio as he squeezed the trigger on the joystick.

Inside the vault chamber, Thunder fired with a deafening roar that was amplified by the echo off the concrete walls. The sabot shell left the gun barrel followed by a tongue of flame. The two sections of the outer-boot fell away leaving only a depleted uranium steel penetrator rod and a rocket motor flying toward the target. The shell's stabilizing fins unfolded. "Away," said Thunder.

The tip of the penetrator hit the vault door at just over Mach One and the rocket motor ignited increasing its speed, pushing it even further. The kinetic energy peeled through the outer steel layers and punched a one-inch diameter hole in the vault door. The penetrator made it through twenty-eight inches of the world's hardest steel before it stopped like a nail that hit a knot in a piece of wood. The penetrator did not break apart. It just stopped inside the vault door, plugging the hole it had just made.

The concrete floor and walls inside the vault chamber shuddered violently from the shell's impact on the steel door like a gong hitting a bell. There was a dull crack that emerged from each of the vault doors followed by a series of pops. "What's that?" said one of the engineers.

"Each of the vault doors has a plate of glass inside that triggers twelve six-inch diameter locking cylinders if the glass is ever broken. The cylinders lock the vault door permanently in place and the only way to open it again it to cut the door open which can take days," said Corporal Wright. "The vibration from the shell's explosion just broke the glass in all eight vault doors and those series of pops you heard were the cylinders locking in place."

"So, we're fucked?"

"Not hardly," said Wright with a smile.

"All units, this is Coyote Six. Everyone stay put," said Turner over the radio.

As the smoke and dust cleared, Turner walked over to the vault door, pulled out a pocket flashlight and inspected the hole. "Red Badger One, this is Six. You are clear. Hit it again. Out," said Turner over the radio as he walked back around the corner.

Thunder's targeting system used the center of the hole to align its next shot. It was a difficult shot like hitting the head of a nail with the point of another nail. "Thunder, load sabot," said Cox into his headset.

Inside Thunder, the autoloader loaded another sabot shell and closed gun's breach. "Sabot up," said Thunder over the radio.

Just as before, Cox rechecked the placement of the crosshairs. "Fire in the hole," said Cox over the radio as he squeezed the trigger on the joystick.

Thunder fired again. "Away," said Thunder. This time the second penetrator rod slammed into the back of the first penetrator rod and pushed both all the way through the vault door and into the vault. The two penetrators slammed into one of the vault's storage compartments, cracking open the small steel door. Hundreds of uncut diamonds burst out and tumbled across the vault floor.

Again Turner emerged from around the corner and walked over to the vault door. He used his flashlight to inspect the hole and saw that it went all the way through. "Outstanding," he said to himself.

Turner ordered Corporal Wright to have a look inside. Corporal Wright pulled an endoscope from his rucksack. He fed the distal tip of the long insertion tube into the hole in the vault door. He used the control section of the instrument to remotely control the direction the lens pointed as it entered the vault. He looked around the vault and tilted down to the floor. He moved the flexible tube to the floor and looked around. Something caught his interest. He manipulated the fiber optic lens until it was positioned in front of a large uncut diamond laying on the floor. He used the endoscope's micro-tweezers to grab the diamond.

"What do you think?" said Turner growing impatient.

Corporal Wright retracted the device with the diamond in the micro-tweezers at the end of the tube. The diamond barely fit through the hole. "What do I think?" said Corporal Wright as he opened the tweezers and the diamond dropped into the palm of his hand. He smiled and said, "I think we are all about to be very rich."

The team members approached. Corporal Wright handed over the diamond and the team members passed it around with smiles and laughs. "I want that back when you are all done drooling over it," said Turner. "No souvenirs until we divide the take."

Turner let his men celebrate for almost two minutes before he barked and ordered them back to work. He wanted them to realize there was a pot of gold at the end of the rainbow and that he had kept his word to them. Everyone on the team had a role to play in order for the mission to succeed. He needed their cooperation until the very end.

TWENTY

It took Thunder the better part of an hour to pierce the seven remaining vaults. The routine was the same each time – line up in front of the vault, then back away as far as possible to give the sabot's boot enough space to separate from the penetrator rod and avoid any damage from the explosions' overpressure.

In the end, there was a one-inch hole in each vault doors. Except for the burn marks, it really didn't look like much damage had been done to the vaults.

Thunder moved out of the way and the four engineers took over the operation. They ran the eight fire hoses through the tunnel and over to each of the vaults. They opened another case and pulled out eight custom-made nozzle clamps for the end of each hose. Each hose's nozzle was centered over the hole on each of the vault doors. The clamps had magnetic attachment arms that held the hose firmly clamped against the door's steel surface. The engineers used a series of worm gears to align and lower each nozzle until it tightly covered the hole in each door.

When the final nozzle was in place, Corporal Wright radioed De Jong, "Let 'em rip."

In the office building basement next to the exposed water main, De Jong opened the valve for each one of the Storz couplers. Meijer started the engine on each one of the portable pumps and the fire hoses filled with water.

In the vault chamber, excess water squirted from each of the holes in the vault doors. The engineers made adjustments in the clamps until most of the water traveled through the holes and into the vaults. Each of the vaults was air-tight and began to fill with water. Each nozzle also had a small metal tube that allowed air to escape from inside the vault as the water filled the space inside.

Seeing that everything was under control and operating as planned, Turner spoke into his radio, "This is Coyote Six. Everyone grab some grub and get some shut-eye if you need it. I don't wanna hear any bitching when we are go again. Red Badger One, you're got guard duty. Over."

"Copy Red Badger One on guard duty, Coyote Six. Out," said Cox over the radio.

The team members moved off, talking amongst themselves about what they would do with their share of the take once the diamonds had been fenced and the laundered money divided. Turner was convinced his men would follow him anywhere at this point.

Outside the facility, the Belgian soldiers watched and waited. There was nothing to do. Nobody dared go down the ramp knowing the rogue Americans had surely set up an ambush or a booby trap.

"We're blind out here. We need to take a look down that ramp," said Tien to Peeters.

"I am not willing to risk more lives just because you lack patience," said Peeters.

"It's not about patience. They are up to something and we need to know what it is," said Tien. "Does the SWAT team have a bomb disposal robot?"

"They do," said Peeters. "And they are not anxious to lose it."

"If I get General Hanson to take responsibility for the robot if it is damaged will they loan it to us?"

"I would imagine they would," said Peeters.

Thirty minutes later a Belgian bomb disposal robot moved down the ramp. A small camera on the end of its articulated arm recorded its progress.

Tien and Peeters watched over the shoulder of the robot's operator. The operator used the robot's remote controls and camera monitor to guide the robot past any debris still on the ramp. It came to the loading dock.

The robot moved over to and climbed a set of stairs on the right side of the loading dock. It moved through the breach and into the tunnel. It was dark. A light mounted on the robot's chassis turned on illuminating the tunnel.

Sitting in the comfort of the hotel penthouse, Cox watched the little robot advancing down the dark tunnel. The ROW's targeting system had already identified the approaching threat and had aligned the crosshairs of the gun's sight over the center of the robot. Cox was disappointed. He wanted more of a challenge. *This is the best they can send?* he thought. He radioed Turner for approval to engage. He didn't want to take any action without Turner's say so. "Nuke the little bastard," said Turner over the radio. Cox squeezed the trigger on the ROW's joystick.

At the end of the tunnel, the ROW opened fire. The sound of the 50-cal machine gun firing was deep and its echo boomed off the concrete walls. It was slower than the Thunder's minigun, but its large caliber bullets were far deadlier.

The ROW's bullets ripped the little robot apart. Pieces flew everywhere. What remained after a three-second barrage was hardly recognizable.

The camera monitor caught the muzzle flashes of the first three rounds from the ROW, then turned to static. The SWAT team operator turned to Tien and said, "You owe us one robot, Lieutenant."

Tien nodded with a weak smile.

After an hour and a half rest break, Turner called everyone on the team back to work. The engineers pulled out a jackhammer and broke the concrete in front of each vault door. There was no hope of tunneling under the door or through the vault walls. They were all designed to withstand such amateur attempts. The engineers were not attempting to go deep into the concrete floor, but rather clearing a path in front of each vault door.

It took three hours before all the eight vaults were filled with water. The engineers shut off the water feeding the fire hoses and removed the nozzles clamped to the vault doors. They temporary plugged the holes in the doors with a heavy-duty mechanical rubber plug that expanded when a bolt in the center of each plug was turned with a wrench. The water stopped leaking from the vault.

The engineers opened another case and removed three fifteen-foot flexible tubes just under the diameter of the hole in each vault door. Each tube was packed with a roll of C-4 plastic explosive. It was a similar setup to the detcord but with twenty-times the explosive punch. The tubes were designed to shear the concrete and steel supports of a four-lane bridge. A blasting cap was pushed into the explosive-clay on the end of each tube. The two-strand wire attached to each blasting cap led to an electronic detonator.

The engineers removed the plug in the first vault door and slid the three C-4 tubes through the hole into the vault leaving only the detonation wires hanging out of the hole. They pushed the rubber plug back in the hole and gently turned the expansion bolt, careful not to damage the wire leads. Everyone cleared the vault chamber and Corporal Wright said, "Fire-in-the-hole" over the radio before pressing the button on the electronic detonator. The explosion rocked the facility.

The water inside the vault super-heated from the kinetic energy generated by the explosion and expanded in a fraction of a second creating an incredible amount of pressure inside the vault. All of the steel compartment doors that held the trays of diamonds cracked open in an instant. Most of the diamonds were undamaged by the explosion and poured out of the compartments. A few diamonds with major flaws cracked into pieces.

The vault door did not breach. It was locked down and the engineers had no hope of breaking the twelve steel cylinders free from the vault's doorframe. Instead, the entire vault doorframe burst from the concrete and steel walls that held it in place leaving a gap and exposing the inside of the vault. A gouge was torn into the concrete floor where the bottom of the vault doorframe had moved and lifted up over the concrete the jackhammers had broken. Some of the anchor bolts that previously held the doorframe in place were sheared and others had chunks of concrete still around them. Water poured out of the vault and into the chamber. It flowed down the hallways and dissipated through the facility.

The engineers opened more cases and retrieved three heavy-duty electric chain winches. It took three engineers to lift one winch. The winches were designed to assist an Abrams tank out of a ditch if required. Each winch had a 30-ton capacity and was made up of multiple steel chains attached to a hook on either end. The chain links were fed through a series of spoked-gears operated by an electric motor.

One of the engineers found the electrical room. He entered and removed the front plate on the main electrical panel. He shut down the power to the facility. He tied-in a 3-phase power extension cable to the electrical panel and turned the power to the facility back on. The extension cable led to a portable electrical panel with three outlets which in turn powered the cables that powered the winches.

The engineers attached an end of the winch hooks to three of the anchor bolts that were still attached to the vault doorframe. The other end of the winch chain was attached to the door of the vault across the chamber. They activated the winches and the breached vault doorframe was slowly pulled open until a man could slide inside the vault.

Several technicians slid into the vault. Their eyes widened when they saw the piles of diamonds that had poured out of the broken compartments and collected in mounds on the vault floor. Like children in a candy store they laughed and joked with each other as they used small gardening shovels to sift through the compartment wreckage and scoop up the diamonds into heavy-duty rubber bags. They used crowbars to pry open any compartment doors that were still partially intact. When a rubber bag was filled to capacity it was sealed and handed out through the gap. They filled eleven bags from just the one vault. The rubber bags were stored in the office building basement for protection from the explosions.

The engineers repeated the breaching operation for each of the seven remaining vaults. It took five hours to clean out all of the vaults. They had filled eighty-six rubber bags of diamonds with a black-market value in excess of five billion dollars.

Their fence would charge twenty percent to sell the uncut stones, but that still left four billion dollars for the team. Of course, the sale wouldn't happen overnight. It would take years to sell that quantity of stolen diamonds. Many of the buyers would be unaware that they were buying stolen merchandise, while others would simply turn a blind eye. With the stigma of blood diamonds, the successful traders of uncut diamonds required that their buyers not ask too many questions about the origin of the stones. Questions simply caused the price of the merchandise to rise until any transaction became prohibitive for a nosy buyer. It was an ethically-challenged, but effective system.

The team was exhausted by the end of the operation, and sluggish. Turner decided to let them rest and eat some chow before continuing with the next phase of the plan. They would need their strength and more importantly... their wits. It was time for Thunder to make its run.

Tien approached Peeters. "Captain Peeters, I've been studying the map you gave me of the area. It looks like there are tunnels leading from the four exchanges to the vaults," said Tien.

"There are two tunnels connecting the exchanges on each side of the square."

"So, why don't you send a reconnaissance team and have a look?"

"After the destruction of the robot, the owners of the exchanges threatened to hold the Belgian government liable for any loses if we enter the facility."

"That's insane."

"They believe the vaults are impenetrable. I have orders not to send anyone inside the facility."

"So, we're just supposed to sit here until they come out?"

"That is the plan at this point."

"Can you at least send reconnaissance teams to watch over the tunnel entrances?"

"My commander says, 'No.' Nobody goes near the tunnels. We watch from a distance."

"Hell of a way to run a war."

"Let's hope it doesn't come to that," said Peeters.

Break time was over and Turner was ready to get moving again. "This is Coyote Six. Everyone up off your asses and let's finish this thing," said Turner over the radio. "I want a neat and orderly line in front of the access chamber according to your assigned number. Out."

Four MPs formed the rear guard and kept watch down the tunnels as the rest of the team members walked through the shallow tunnel into the basement of the office building. One of the engineers brought in a case and opened it. The case contained dozens of home-made breathing devices made from plastic soda bottles, rubber tubing, and a sawed-off snorkel mouthpiece. They were simple devices that provided three minutes of air. Each team member picked up a breathing device and formed a line in front of the exposed water main.

Turner moved to the front of the line and picked up an empty rubber bag. "You have one chance to come clean and drop any of the stones you stole from your team into the bag. If I catch anyone with even one karat, I will personally shoot you in the balls. Are we clear?" said Turner pulling out his pistol.

The team responded with a lackluster "Hooah." Turner walked down the line and the team members dropped the stones they had hidden in various parts of their bodies into the rubber bag. One of the technicians only dropped three stones that he had hidden in his mouth. Turner stopped and waited beside the man. "I am not above doing a cavity search if I feel anyone is not obeying my order," said Turner without making eye-contact.

The technician put his hand into the back of his pants and reached down. With a painful look on his face, he produced a balloon filled with twenty diamonds and a smell that made even Turner wince. "Nice, Specialist. Very nice," said Turner as the Specialist empty the contents of the balloon into the rubber bag.

Turner continued down the line until everyone had given up their diamonds. He was pretty sure that a few of his men still had some hidden diamonds on them, but he didn't have time to do a systematic search of each team member. He realized early on that he had turned his men into traitors and thieves. As much as it gulled him, Turner would let the infractions slide. Staying focused on the mission was important, especially at this phase. "Everyone leave your body armor, web belts, and weapons in this room. You will not need them on the other side. If you are stopped and searched by police, you do not want a weapon discovered on your person. They will arrest you and you will not be able to enjoy the fruits of your labor. A grenade or weapon that is accidentally discharged inside the pipe will ruin not only your day but that of those that have not yet made the journey. A web belt or body armor can catch on a bad weld inside the pipe and you will drown. Everything stays behind," said Turner.

The men stacked their weapon, belts and body armor. Corporal Wright controlled the water main. He closed the main's shutoff valve, then opened the access hatch. The first passenger crawled inside and placed the home-made breathing apparatus in his mouth. He tested the device by taking a deep breath and gave a thumbs up to Corporal Wright. "Passenger One up," said Corporal Wright over his radio headset as he closed the access hatch and opened the shutoff valve. He watched through the glass portal as the first man was swept away by the flood of water entering the pipeline. "One away," said Corporal Wright into his radio.

Three blocks away, in the basement of an apartment building, Visser and two men watched the glass portal of an identical access hatch. The first passenger entered the access chamber and was stopped by a Kevlar net on the far end of the tube. The two men closed the shutoff valve and opened the access hatch. They helped the first passenger climb out and handed him a towel. "One arrived safely," said Visser into his radio headset.

The passenger pulled off his breathing mask and laughed. "That was the thrill of a lifetime," he said.

Back in the office building basement, Corporal Wright loaded up the next man in line and launched him through the tube.

Once there was an even number of men on both sides of the pipeline, Turner gave the order to launch the rubbers bags filled with diamonds. Each bag was launched separate so they did not bunch up and clog the pipe.

The bags were caught by the Kevlar net on the opposite end and fished out of the chamber by the men waiting on the other side. It took an hour to launch and retrieve all the bags. Visser kept a close watch on the bags to ensure that none of the soldiers on this side of the pipeline tampered with the bags' contents.

Billy and Lowell watched the square through the diamond exchange window. "This is crazy," said Lowell. "Just sitting here watching."

"I've been thinking," said Billy. "Why build the vaults underground?"

"Safer, I suppose. People can't see what you're doing."

"So, how do they get the diamonds to the exchanges and back again?"

"What do you mean?"

"Doesn't seem very safe transferring diamonds by foot. And the exchanges aren't far enough to warrant an armored truck."

"So, what are you thinking? Some sort of tunnel from the exchanges to the vaults?"

"It's what I would do if I were them. Keeps everything safe from ambush and out of the public eye."

"The Belgian forces must know if there are tunnels. Why haven't they sent someone to check them out?"

"No idea. But then again, I ain't Belgian."

"So, let's check out the basement and see if you're right."

"Okay… but there's one other thing…"

"What's that?"

"Why would you run a cable on the outside of a luxury hotel? Kinda messes up the aesthetics of the place, ya know?

"What the hell are you talking about?"

"Across the square… the top floor of that hotel," said Billy pointing. "How is Thunder controlled from a distance?"

"The control station uses a microwave antenna array."

"Does it look something like that?" said Billy pointing to the microwave antenna array on the rooftop of the hotel.

"Holy shit! That's it!" said Lowell moving toward the front door. "Aren't you coming?"

"You're the only one that can stop Thunder. I'll check out the basement and see if I can find that tunnel."

"Okay," said Lowell, unsure, "You watch your top knot, Billy."

"You too, Lowell," said Billy moving to the basement stairs.

Once the bags of diamonds had arrived safely at the opposite end of the pipeline, Turner ordered the men to resume their escape through the access chamber. Corporal Wright loaded and launched the next man in line. Turner radioed Cox, "Red Badger One, this is Coyote Six. Over."

"Go ahead, Coyote Six. Over."

"Red Badger One, you may begin your run. Give 'em hell, son. Coyote Six, out."

TWENTY-ONE

Lowell crouched down by the corner of the exchange doorway as he called Tien on his mobile phone. "Lieutenant, I think I may have something. I'm heading across the square to check it out. Make sure those Belgian soldiers hold their fire, will ya?"

"Yes, of course," said Tien. "What are you checking out, Staff Sergeant? And where is your brother?" There was no answer. Lowell had hung up.

Tien warned the Belgian troops and watched as Lowell ran across the square to the hotel. "Man's got a hole in his chest. How does he do that?" said Tien to herself.

A Griffon sat parked at the top of the ramp with its machine gun pointed into the dark hole that was once the secured loading dock. The Griffon's gunner watched the video monitor from inside the armored vehicle. He saw a slight shimmer in the darkness, but couldn't make out anything solid. He switched the remote targeting system to thermal and saw the red and orange outline of Thunder. It was the last thing he saw before a HEAT round hit the front of the Griffon and exploded killing everyone inside.

Lowell was halfway across the square when he heard the explosion and instinctively dove to the ground. He correctly identified the sound of the explosion as a HEAT round and imagined that Thunder was heading up the ramp. He was in the open with no cover anywhere near. If Thunder's targeting system spotted him, he was a dead man.

Thunder fired a second high explosive round at the Griffon. The explosion ignited the gas tank and the secondary explosion launched the 20-ton Griffon through the air. It landed on its side and was engulfed in flames. It no longer blocked the ramp.

Thunder raced up to the top of the loading ramp and stopped. The concrete sides of the loading ramp still protected Thunder from any enemy fire on its flanks.

The Belgian A109 helicopter turned toward the ramp. It fired its rockets and opened fire with its machine gun.

The ramp walls were thick but quickly disintegrated against the hail of rockets and gunfire. A chunk of concrete fell away revealing the top of Thunder. It's minigun already lined up through the crevice, opened fire at the helicopter.

The helicopter's cockpit windshield was pitted with bullet holes. The barrage of bullets killed both the pilot and the co-pilot. The helicopter spun out of control.

Lowell watched as the helicopter headed straight at him. He jumped up and made a run for the hotel. The helicopter crashed in the square where he had been laying. The helicopter's rotor blades cut into the cobblestones, knocking them loose and kicking them into the air. Lowell ran into the hotel as shrapnel from the crash rained down.

Billy was approaching the bottom of the basement stairs when he heard the explosions. The building shook. At the end of a hallway, he saw an armored door with an electronic lock. He approached.

A gun pressed up against the back of his head. A guard that had moved up behind him spoke in Dutch. Billy didn't know what the man was saying, but he figured it was something like put your hands in the air. Billy raised his hands. The guard pushed him against the wall and searched him for weapons. As the guard reached down to search Billy's boots, Billy elbowed him in the face. The guard fell backward. Billy turned and kicked him in the face with his boot. The guard fell to the floor unconscious.

Billy picked up the guard's machine gun and slung it over his shoulder. He picked up his pistol and stuck it under his belt. He moved to the door. It was locked. Billy moved back over to the guard and slapped him awake. Billy pointed the barrel of the machine gun at the guard's head and motioned from him to open the door. The guard obeyed and opened the door. Billy used the guard's handcuffs to secure the man's wrist to a radiator. He searched the guard, found his keys and threw them down the hallway out of the guard's reach.

With the machine gun leveled, Billy moved through the doorway and into the dark tunnel...

In the square, Thunder emerged from the ramp and engaged the two remaining Griffons with its main cannon and the soldiers with its minigun. Thunder's reactive camouflage constantly changed to match the background and made it difficult to see as it moved. Only the bursts of flame from its cannon and minigun were clear and marked its location. Small arms bullets bounced off the drone's composite armor. Thunder crabbed sideways and pivoted in fast arcs as it lined up its main cannon with the Griffons, and fired.

The drone's auto-targeting system was deadly accurate and destroy both armored vehicles within the first thirty seconds of the battle.

Next, Thunder's minigun swept around the square picking off any soldiers that were brave enough to raise their heads from cover and fire at the drone.

A fire team unleashed a shoulder-held anti-tank missile at the drone. Thunder launched flares, smoke and chaff canisters creating a cloud of confusion. The missile lost its guidance signal but kept flying at its target's last known position. The drone pivoted and crouched. The missile flew past Thunder and exploded in the doorway of the exchange where Billy and Lowell had been hiding. Thunder's minigun targeted and killed both soldiers before they could prepare a second missile. The Belgians were no match for Thunder.

Tien kept her head down and hid behind the front of a car where she knew the car's engine would most likely protect her. The minigun sprayed the car with shells and shattered its windows, but the bullets did not penetrate to the opposite side. Peeters was not so lucky and was hit several times. He went down, badly wounded.

Having eliminated all immediate threats, Thunder left the square and took off down the street with incredible speed.

Tien watched with disbelief as the drone once again disappeared. She imagined that the diamonds were hidden somewhere inside Thunder. Tien heard Peeters moan in pain and moved to his side. She did her best to stop the bleeding before a medic arrived. Tien looked out at the carnage and knew she was on her own.

Inside the penthouse, Cox was laughing as he sat behind the drone's controls and watched the video monitors. An image on one of the monitors caught his eye – It was Billy moving down the tunnel straight toward a ROW machine gun. Cox set Thunder's controls on auto and grabbed the joystick that controlled the ROW machine gun. The auto-targeting system had already identified Billy as a threat and had aligned the crosshairs of the machine gun's optical sight on Billy's head. Cox smiled as he squeezed the trigger.

Lowell kicked open the door to the penthouse and leveled his pistol at Cox. "Give me a reason to kill you, Cox. Anything will do," said Lowell.

Cox froze. Lowell approached and hit Cox over the head with the butt of his pistol. Cox crumpled falling out of the chair to the floor. Lowell rolled him out of the way, sat down, switched off the ROW's auto-targeting system and took control of Thunder.

Thunder slowed to a stop on the street. It turned and headed back toward the square.

Lowell did not notice Cox waking up. Cox reached for a pistol he had hidden under the seat of the chair. He raised the pistol to the back of Lowell's head.

Lowell caught a glimpse of Cox in the reflection of the monitors. He shifted his head as Cox fired twice. The bullet shattered one of the screens.

Three more shots rang out and Cox went down. His blood soaked into the carpet as he died.

Lowell turned to see Tien in the doorway holding her smoking pistol. Lowell smiled and said, "Thanks, L.T."

"It's Lieutenant, Staff Sergeant," said Tien.

"Whatever you say, ma'am."

"Do we have it? Do we have Thunder?" said Tien, hopeful.

"Damn right we do," said Lowell.

"I think they hid the diamonds in it. Bring it back to the square and we'll check it out," said Tien.

"Wilco… Lieutenant," said Lowell.

Back in the office building basement, as the line of passengers thinned to the final few, Turner radioed the four MPs guarding the tunnels to rendezvous at the access hatch.

The MPs moved through the shallow tunnel into the office building basement. They removed their web belts and body armor and stacked them along with their weapons. Corporal Wright loaded and launched the final four MPs through the water main. Like the others, Turner rid himself of weapon, belt, and body armor. He entered the chamber and placed a breathing apparatus in his mouth. "Don't forget me, Master Sergeant," said Corporal Wright as he closed the access hatch and opened the shutoff valve.

Turner was whisked away by the flood of water entering the chamber. Once Corporal Wright received word that Turner had arrived on the other end of the pipeline, Corporal Wright picked up one of the remaining breathing devices, climbed into the chamber and closed the access hatch. There were two wheels inside the chamber designed for the final passenger. He turned the first and the access hatch locked from the inside. He turned the second and the shutoff valve opened and flooded the chamber. He was carried away down the pipe.

On the opposite end, Corporal Wright arrived inside the second chamber and hit the Kevlar net. Another engineer closed the valve and opened the access hatch. Corporal Wright climbed out and was congratulated by the others. Turner ordered the engineer to close the access hatch and open the shutoff valve. Turner didn't want the water company to track down the blockage point. Not yet, anyway. Soon it wouldn't matter. Everything had worked as planned.

Billy walked into the vault chamber and examined the breached vaults. The floor was covered with almost a foot of water. For the most part, he understood what had happened. Turner and his team had used Thunder to pierce the vaults. He didn't understand why there was water on the floor, but it really didn't matter at this point. They were gone and so were the diamonds. He saw the endoscope, abandoned on the floor. He picked it up, wrapped it in a loop and stuck it in his jacket pocket. His mobile phone rang and he answered it. "It's Lowell. We've got Thunder," said Lowell over the phone.

"That's great, Lowell," said Billy. "And the diamonds?"

"No. We searched the drone and they're not there. Turner must have 'em. Any sign of him?"

"Nope. He and his men are gone."

"I might be able to help with that. Can your CIA guy track a mobile phone?"

"Yeah. Do you have his mobile number?"

"Maybe. Remember that guy on the roof that you conked on the head with that brick?"

"Yeah."

"I grabbed his mobile and it's only got one number in. I'm guessing its Turner's."

"And you're just telling me this now?"

"I forgot. I've kinda been busy, ya know."

"Text me the number and I'll forward it along with your number. If they get something, they'll call you."

"Where are you gonna be?" said Billy.

"I still got a few things I want to check out," said Lowell.

Billy hung up and moved cautiously through the shallow tunnel into the office building basement. He saw the hole in the far wall and the exposed water main with its access chamber. As he approached the chamber he saw the remaining breathing apparatuses and picked one up for a closer look. Everything clicked in his mind. How they had escaped. He was angry and frustrated. Evil had won. It was the same feeling he had had when the Nomad had escaped after killing his lover. And just like then… he couldn't let it stand. He moved to the access chamber and studied it. He closed the shutoff valve and opened the hatch…

The team members placed the rubber bags into six large canvas bags and stacked the canvas bags on a table at the end of the room. Visser was busy working on something inside an open canvas bag already on the table. "Fall in," said Turner.

The team member fell into line in front of Turner standing with Visser behind the table holding the canvas bags carrying the diamonds and the bag Visser had brought with him. "You men were chosen for a reason. As expected, you have performed your mission with determination and skill. And you have survived. Ya know… there's only one problem with partners in an enterprise such as this one, and it's not sharing out the spoils. There is more than enough for everyone to enjoy a life of leisure for multiple lifetimes. No. The only problem is getting everyone to keep their fucking mouths shut," said Turner. He reached into the open bag, picked something up in each hand and raised both his hands.

The men on the opposite side of the table were soldiers and had all been through basic training. They recognized the detonators in Turner's hands and were familiar with the detonation sequence. Turner pressed each of the detonators' buttons three times.

The bag that Visser had brought and set on the table contained two Claymore mines set up on tripods inside the bag. They had been positioned so they were facing away from Visser and Turner. The shaped charges inside the mines exploded outward launching one thousand four hundred steel ball bearings into the room and shredding all of the surviving team members. "Outstanding," said Turner. "Now that's what I would call a well-designed weapon."

A few of the men were still alive and groaned in pain. Turner and Visser walked through the bodies and shot every man in the head to ensure that dead men tell no tales.

"All right. Let's get a move on," said Turner.

They each slid one of the bags on their backs like a pack and carried the other four. They exited the room.

Billy slammed into the Kevlar net inside the second access chamber. He saw light through the glass portal and could see the outline of the hatch door. What he didn't see were the two wheels that controlled the shutoff valve and opened the hatch from the inside. Since this chamber would always have someone manning it from the outside, there had been no need to design the two wheels on the inside of the pipe. Billy was stuck and running out of air. He pulled out the pistol and fire a round into the glass. The glass shattered but stayed in place with only a small hole to relieve the water pressure. He fired two more rounds into the glass with the same result. The glass stayed intact. His breathing apparatus ran out of air. He pulled it from his mouth. He used the tip of his boot to kick the glass until it finally broke outward. Water flooded out, but the water level inside the pipe did not lower. He was starting to feel faint from lack of oxygen. He knew if he passed out, his life was over.

He reached through the broken portal with his arm and found the shutoff valve. He closed the valve and the water stopped flowing and the water level lowered. He reached in the opposite direction for the wheel that opened the hatch, but couldn't find it. It was too far away to reach. He could breathe again, but he was still trapped inside the water main.

He reached into his jacket pocket and pulled out the endoscope. He fed the lens end of the tube through the portal and looked around the room. He saw all the dead bodies of the team laying on the floor. *Jesus*, he thought. He turned the controls on the endoscope until the lens faced the chamber access hatch and he saw the wheel that opened the hatch. He manipulated the tube closer to the wheel and opened the micro-tweezers. They were not nearly wide enough to grab the wheel.

He stopped and thought for a moment. He manipulated the tube end so it snaked its way through the wheel and wrapped the end around one of the wheel supports. He pulled on the endoscope and heard the wheel move. He repeated the process until the hatch opened. He pushed the hatch out of the way and it clanged loudly against the pipe.

Turner and Visser were almost to the apartment building's back exit door when they heard the faint clang of the hatch hitting the water main pipe. They exchanged a surprised look. "Are you sure you put a bullet in everyone on your side of the room?" said Turner.

"What make you think it was me that missed?" said Visser.

"Because I don't miss," said Turner. "I'll get the car and load up the diamonds. You go back and take care of your unfinished business."

"How do I know you will be here when I return?"

"If I wanted you dead, you'd already be dead. Like I said, there is plenty to go around for those that can keep their mouths shut and obey orders. Besides, I don't speak Dutch in case we are questioned by the police."

Visser nodded and dropped his bags. Turner moved toward the exit door. Visser pulled out his pistol and moved back through the apartment building toward the basement.

Billy climbed out of the chamber. He was soaking wet and grabbed one of the remaining towels. He kept his pistol leveled as he walked through the bodies on the floor. Billy stopped when he heard the hinges on basement door as it opened.

With his pistol drawn Visser entered the basement. He wasn't looking for a confrontation but wanted to ensure there was no one still alive. The men they had betrayed were trained killers. He wanted to spend the rest of his life enjoying the money he had earned, not looking over his shoulder.

The basement was still and silent. Everything seemed the same as when they had left it. He moved further inside. He knelt down and checked each one of the bodies to ensure that it was indeed dead. They were all dead. He kept his eyes on the room looking for any movement. There was none. He glanced over at the access chamber. The hatch was closed. He noticed the portal window was broken and glass was on the floor which meant it was broken from the inside. The water was not flowing through the pipeline as they had left it. He moved closer to look inside the chamber through the broken portal. He saw nothing inside. He opened the hatch. Still nothing.

Visser did not notice Billy as he slid out from inside the pipe segment that had been cut out of the main water pipe and discarded to one side of the basement. Billy took aim. He wanted to shoot the man, but he couldn't be sure he was part of the team that robbed the vaults. He had checked each of the men on the floor to see if they were alive. He could be an undercover cop. Billy needed to find out the man's intentions. "Don't move," said Billy.

Visser froze. "Lay your weapon on the floor, kneel down and put your hands behind your head," said Billy. "Any sudden moves and I will shoot you."

Visser knew that Billy was not a Belgian police officer because of his accent and he was speaking English not Dutch. He also thought he was not a survivor from the team. If he was a survivor, he surely would have shot Visser already. *No, this man is someone else,* thought Visser. "You are American?" said Visser as he slowly lowered his pistol to the floor.

"Shut up and do as I say," said Billy.

"Did you do all of this?" said Visser as he knelt and put his hands behind his head. "Kill all these men?"

"They were all dead when I arrived. Who are you?" said Billy as he pulled himself out of the pipe segment.

As Billy shifted his weight the heavy pipe started to roll. Billy reached out with both hands to stabilize himself.

Visser grabbed his pistol off the floor and fired at Billy. He missed Billy's head by a few inches. Billy ducked back into the pipe. Bullets ricocheted off the outside of the pipe making it clang inside. The steel walls of the pipe were too thick for the bullets to penetrate.

Billy was trapped and knew it was only a matter of a few moments before the man moved to an angle where he could fire into the pipe. *It'll be easy pickings,*

Billy thought. *He'll just shoot into the pipe and let the ricocheting bullets do all the work. I'm a dead man if I don't do something fast.* Billy used his left foot to slide off his right boot. He kicked the empty boot down to the opposite end of the pipe. It slid part of the way out of the pipe and caught Visser's attention. Visser fired hitting the boot twice. Billy yanked himself out of the pipe and shot Visser three times in the chest. Visser crumpled to the ground and dropped his pistol. He drowned to death as his lungs filled with blood.

TWENTY-TWO

Turner had reentered the apartment building when he heard the gunshots. He stood in the hallway near the exit where Visser had dropped his bags. He planned to kill Visser like the rest when he returned. He didn't like loose ends. Hearing the gunshots, he wondered if Visser was already dead. Turner was no coward. He thought about going back to the basement to see what had happened but decided against it. Instead, he picked up the bags and exited the building. He would live with the fact that Visser could be out there somewhere hunting for him. It was an acceptable risk.

Turner walked out into the sunlight and over to a Mercedes that was parked near the building exit. He loaded Visser's bags into the trunk with his three bags already inside. He closed the trunk lid and climbed into the driver's seat. He adjusted the mirror to the way he liked it. He was not in a hurry. He had won. It was time to relax. Turner dialed his mobile phone. A man answered. "Mission accomplished, sir," said Turner.

"Well done, Master Sergeant," said the man.

"Thank you, sir. It was a brilliant plan. I will see you soon," said Turner and hung up.

Turner started the engine and slipped the gearshift into Drive. He released the parking brake and steered the sedan into the street.

As he drove toward the end of the street, he noticed a shimmer through the windshield. At first, he thought it a glimmer of sunlight as the sun was low on the horizon. Slowly, it occurred to him that the shimmer was no natural phenomenon. His fear was confirmed when a panel opened and a 120mm gun barrel appeared floating several feet off the street... pointing straight at him. It fired.

A long plume of flame followed the sabot shell as it left the end of the gun tube. The sabot's boot fell away after the first twenty feet and the rocket motor ignited increasing the shell's speed to Mach-2. The penetrator rod punched a neat hole in the windshield and passed through the glass without incident. It hit Turner in the center of the chest and snapped his vertebrae as it passed through his body and out the back of the sedan. The penetrator hit one of the bags and carried a few diamonds with it as it punched a hole through the back of the trunk. The diamonds tumbled onto the street. The Mercedes slowed as Turner's foot fell off the accelerator. It hit Thunder head-on. The reactive camouflage flickered off and Thunder appeared, but no real damage was done.

Turner was still alive when the airbag deployed hitting him in the face. A few seconds later he died, a very rich man.

Lowell sat in the penthouse behind Thunder's controls and watched the video monitors. "Outstanding," he said with a wry smile.

Billy sat on the patio of a biergarten finishing his first beer – a dark Roggenbier made from rye. Tien and Lowell approached. "Is Thunder on its way?" said Billy as they sat down.

"It will be in about an hour," said Lowell.

"I would have thought you'd be traveling with it," said Billy.

"Yeah, me too. But I've got a new assignment," said Lowell.

"Wait a minute… you're retiring in a few months," said Billy.

"Not anymore. The United States Army in its infinite wisdom has decided to give me a promotion. I'll be in for few more years."

"What prompted that?" said Billy. "Army that happy to have Thunder back?"

"That and… my new commanding officer put in a good word," said Lowell motioning to Tien.

"Lowell's gonna work for you?" said Billy.

"Yep. Somebody's gotta keep him out of trouble," said Tien.

"Good luck with that," said Billy. "So what exactly are you gonna be doing for the good lieutenant?"

"Captain. I received a promotion too," said Tien. "Sergeant First Class Gamble will be operating undercover on his first assignment. The inspector general is not convinced that Master Sergeant Turner acted alone and frankly neither am I. With Sergeant

Gamble we can start at the bottom and work our way up without raising a lot of suspicions. Hopefully, we'll find the bastards that did this."

"Nobody expects a grunt," said Lowell.

"I suppose congratulations are in order. Can I buy you two a beer?" said Billy.

"Absolutely. You can get me one of them Doppelbocks," said Lowell.

"No thank you. We're still on duty," said Tien.

Lowell looked disappointed but didn't say anything. "Seriously, Captain?" said Billy.

"Ah hell. I'll have a Hefeweizen," said Tien.

Billy ordered. "Kind of a pussy beer, Captain," said Lowell.

Billy winced.

Tien steamed. "So, where are you off to, Billy?" she said, changing the subject.

"Copenhagen for a few weeks, then… I don't know," said Billy.

"Heading back to the ranch for Christmas?" said Lowell.

"Not this year. Culper lets me wander where I want as long as I don't return to the U.S."

"Hardly seems fair. You just did a great service to your country," said Tien.

"Yeah, well… Culper's not really into 'fair.' Still, it's nice. Helping my country. I've spent so many years traveling, I've sort of lost my home. This helps me remember my way back… for some day in the future."

The waitress brought the beer and they enjoyed each other's company for a while longer. Billy glanced at his brother. He wanted to say something more than just goodbye, but he never found the words. Neither did Lowell.

Dear Reader,

Thank you for giving Stealing Thunder: Book 3 of the Nomad Series a try. I hope you enjoyed reading it as much as I enjoyed writing it. Please consider my other series starting with We Stand Alone: Book 1 of the Airman Series.

As always, your review on Amazon.com is most appreciated. I read each one and they help my writing.

If you would like to know when my future books come out please subscribe to my newsletter on my website. You'll also get a free copy of one of my books when you sign up. I won't sell your name or send you too many notices. I reserve my mailing list for announcements about my new novel releases.

http://davidleecorley.com/

Sincerely,

David Lee Corley

My other novels:
- Monsoon Rising
- Prophecies of Chaos
- We Stand Alone
- Café Wars
- Sèvres Protocol

Made in United States
Troutdale, OR
10/22/2023